PIGGY IN THE MIDDLE

Sandra's problems began when she joined the police force. Her boyfriend Dave, a journalist, is on the opposite side of the fence from her – as she soon finds out when they are working on the same 'murder' case. And her work becomes unexpectedly, increasingly difficult.

'An extraordinarily perceptive account of how Sandra finally comes to terms with the stress of her job and her own mistakes . . . all this realism is pure talent . . . it is written with adrenalin for ink.'
Punch

'This mustn't be missed . . .'
Books for Keeps

JAN NEEDLE

Piggy in the Middle

Fontana Lions

First published in Great Britain 1982 by André Deutsch Ltd
First published in Fontana Lions 1983
8 Grafton Street, London W1X 3LA
Second impression September 1985

Fontana Lions is an imprint of Fontana Paperbacks,
a division of the Collins Publishing Group

Printed in Great Britain
by William Collins Sons & Co. Ltd, Glasgow

For Laurie and Lillian

ONE

It seemed odd to Sandra Patterson, when she thought about it later, that while she'd been sitting in headquarters writing up the ball and chain affair, Noor Allahi had been battering his dad to death. Odd, and at first unbelievable. She'd known Noor Allahi for years, although not exactly to talk to. They'd gone to the same school. He was a tiny little fellow, something of a runt. Hidden strength, though, clearly. He'd bashed his father's head in till it had spattered on the walls.

Police work was full of coincidences, and incidents that happened totally at random. That was why she liked it. It was not so much that you did police work; somehow it did you. She often felt, the summer she started, that it was like standing in a river. You were stationary, and events flowed over you. Every day brought something new, something totally unexpected. Or, more often, nothing. It could be a real bind, there was no getting away from that. But it was better than being in a bank. Oh yes.

The afternoon that Noor Allahi killed his dad, one of those coincidences had taken place. She'd seen Allahi, and some other blokes she'd gone to school with, for the first time in ages. They had been Joe Public, she had been The Law. Not a comfortable position for either of them.

It had come at a good time, though, because she was bored out of her skull. She'd been sitting in HQ for what seemed hours, doing filing, and she was hot, and sweaty, and fed up. The station, in Union Street, was a modern one. architect designed in glass and concrete slab. Not only did it look like an abortion, it was a summertime disaster. The rays hit the glass and the temperature rocketed. Terry –

Constable Slater – was with her in the room when the phone rang. He was big, and fat, and red-faced. He was sweating, too. The heat was terrible.

When he'd put the receiver down, he mopped his face and grinned.

'Thank God for that,' he said. 'A chance to get outside. I'll see if Harrison'll let you come along, shall I? Get some air.'

Sandra looked ruefully at the huge pile of paper waiting to be sorted out and stuck away. And smiled.

'Yeah,' she said. 'Great if you could, Terry. Cheers.'

Brian was in the car as well, chatting Sandra lazily. She sat in the back, enjoying the ride, enjoying the sea air blasting through the open windows, enjoying the smells of hot tarmac, diesel smoke, boiling hops from the brewery, even enjoying Brian. The town was bathed in sunshine, full of holiday-makers, bright and cheerful. She was as happy as a lark.

Sandra didn't mind being chatted up by Brian anymore, it rather amused her. Brian or anyone else, for that matter, for she knew it was only a routine. At first, when she'd joined up, she'd been rather scandalised at the flirting that went on, it had been completely unexpected. And she'd still never told her boyfriend, Dave, about it. He was older than she was, and as possessive as they come. He'd have gone mad, hairless. She'd told her sister Maggie, though, who was twenty two and married, and she'd laughed like a drain.

'What d'you expect, my lovely,' she'd said. 'When I worked down at Simpsons it was epidemic. Some of the office ones were the worst, it just depended on the type and opportunity.'

'But it's the police,' said Sandra. She coloured as she said it, because it sounded silly. Sure enough, Maggie laughed.

'Surprise surprise,' she said. 'The police are human beings after all! What did you expect?'

They were sitting in Maggie's front room, on the big settee, watching the rain sliding down the windows. Sandra sighed.

'I dunno really,' she said. 'I mean, I've fancied being in the force for years. I suppose I had this idea . . . Well, I suppose I thought they were different. I mean, on things like that. Moral things, you know.'

'Never mind, love,' said Maggie, seriously. 'Some of the worst ones are the nicest in the end. Roger could be a terror at work, and I married him, didn't I? He's lovely.

'Anyway,' she added. 'It's nice to know you're fancied, whatever anyone says. Ruddy ages since anyone made a pass at me!'

'You'd die of fright!' said Sandra.

'Don't you be so sure, gal,' said Maggie. 'There's life in the old girl yet, you know!'

And they'd laughed.

Terry, who was driving the Panda, made a noise.

'That looks like it,' he said. 'Down past Lister's wall. There's the fire tender.'

They drew up behind it and got out. Sandra stretched her legs in her black tights, longing for the sea air on her skin. She looked out across the small commercial dock, watched the pale blue ferry tootling across the sparkling harbour. Day off tomorrow. Down the beach and keep the good work up on her tan. She longed to be in the cold green water.

'Roll on,' said Terry, good-naturedly. 'They're drunk as monkeys.'

The incident was a typically minor one. They'd only gone along for the ride, if truth were told. A gaggle of apprentices from Lister's Heavy Engineering, the day before the wedding of a mate.

'It's an old custom at Lister's,' Terry told her. 'A stunt. They chuck 'em in the harbour, or tar and feather 'em, or something. This one's got the ball and chain job. Silly sod, he'll get a ball and chain for life in the morning. If he lives.'

Sandra looked curiously at the boy on the ground. He certainly looked as if he might not survive. He was lying on the scrubby grass of the spare ground, his face extremely

3

pale. He looked awful. There was a half empty bottle beside his head. Of rum.

'Drunken oafs,' said Brian, bitterly. He was a very moral copper, Brian. He hated drunks, and trouble-makers, and young hooligans. He looked quite angry, almost savage.

Sandra couldn't help but smile, though. Ill as the boy appeared, he was a real sight for all that. He was dressed up in a sort of furry suit, full-length, with legs and arms and all. Behind his head, there hung a bear mask. No wonder he was sweating, he must be roasted. She felt a pang for his head next morning. Poor devil, he'd be practically unconscious. Strangely, she didn't feel a pang for the bride. Let anyone try a stunt like that on *her*, the day she got married. Just let them try . . .

At the boy's feet were two firemen, one struggling with a hacksaw at the ball and chain. He stopped, panting, when the police arrived.

'It's a fire-station job, this,' he said, wiping his cheek with his hand. 'They've case-hardened the chain and shackle. Engineers! Too clever by half.'

'Which ones were the culprits?' asked Brian. 'We could book 'em if you like, no problem.'

The firemen exchanged glances. The gaggle of youths – some in overalls, some in fancy dress – shuffled uneasily. Sandra thought it queer, as well. Terry laughed.

'They deserve a medal, I'd say,' he said. 'Trying to save young Walter from a fate worse than death.'

'Walter?' said Brian. 'Do you know him?'

'Nah,' said Terry. He sang. 'Walter, Walter, lead me to the altar.'

There was a polite laugh from the apprentices. A grateful one.

The boy on the ground was turning green. The firemen moved back while he was sick, then shifted him slightly, to a cleaner patch.

'Come on, old lad,' said the older, kindly. 'I think we'll take you to the station, burn it off.'

Sandra, a movement in the corner of her eye, looked up.

4

Four other young men in overalls approached from Lister's gate. They were carrying a vice and some clamps. She jumped. She knew them.

Well, three of them, anyway. The leading one, tall with a beard, had been to school with her since a kid. Peter Croxley. He started, when he recognised her.

'Hi, Sandra,' he said, smiling. 'Still with the enemy, are we?'

He said it easily, not meaning any harm, perhaps. They were all stoned, anyway, drunk as lords. Most of the youths had bottles in their hands. Bottles or cans. But Brian's face darkened.

'Just watch it, you,' he said. 'You could be in trouble, Sonny Jim. Just watch your mouth.'

Sandra felt herself going red. She'd only been in the force a few months. It sounded absurd, to her, when her colleagues spoke like that. Like something off the telly.

Terry moved to defuse the situation.

'We take quite a dim view of this, you know,' he said mildly. 'Wastes a lot of public time. The case-hardening was going a bit far. Just stupid.'

Peter – like Terry – was a very easy-going bloke. He smiled broadly back.

'Yeah,' he said. 'Ahmed got carried away. Well, we all did. Sorry.'

Sandra, although she'd known them, had somehow avoided looking at the Asians, perhaps not consciously. But now she had to. Ahmed Rashid. He'd been in the year above her. And Noor Allahi, too. Same age but a different kettle of fish entirely. When he saw her looking, Ahmed smiled. But he didn't speak, he'd know better than to embarrass her like Peter had. Noor Allahi's eyes slid sideways, then down. He shuffled.

'You did it, did you?' asked Brian, nastily. 'This case-hardening?'

Ahmed opened his mouth, but Brian interrupted him.

'Not you,' he said. 'Here, Shorty. I'm talking to you. Did you do this job?'

Noor Allahi looked up, startled.

'No sir,' he mumbled. 'I have not done it. I have not done it.'

He was just the same as he'd been at school. His accent was thick, impenetrable. He'd only come in to England six or seven years ago. Ahmed spoke. His English was perfect, he'd been born in the town. He even had the local accent.

'I did the main job,' he said, looking at Brian. 'I case-hardened the shackle. I'm sorry we've caused all this trouble, though. It was just a bit of fun, meant to be. Sorry.'

He was relaxed, but cautious. He was quite smooth. Brian was still tensed up, beside Sandra. She could feel it. Terry stepped in quickly.

'You're a damned nuisance, the lot of you,' he said. 'You're a pain in the flue. Now clear off back to work, why don't you? Just clear off.'

He'd sharpened his voice, and he put on a fierce expression. Sandra nearly grinned. All the embarrassment of being Them and Us, that Brian made her feel acutely, went away with Terry. If she'd dared, she would have winked at Peter. She looked at him, and he slipped her half a smile. She smiled back, cautiously.

'Take the tools back, lads,' one of the firemen said. 'We'll have to take young Walter here to the station.'

'Make sure they cut the right ball off, Charlie,' someone shouted. Brian, who had turned away, spun back, glaring angrily at them.

'Stop that filth,' he snapped. 'Who said that?'

They looked at each other and shrugged. They began to move away. Peter glanced at Sandra and she turned red again, feeling obscurely angry at Brian. She thought he was being stupid.

That afternoon, back at the station, she was told to write the incident up, as an exercise. She was a fluent writer, and Terry, when he checked her first attempt, laughed out loud.

'God, gal,' he said. 'It's meant to be a report, not a short-story. You couldn't read that out in court. Just write it dull and factual, right?'

And while she sat there, sucking at her pencil in the hot and sticky office, Noor Allahi went back to his home in Hindley Lane End, and killed his father. It was odd.

TWO

David Tanner, Sandra's boyfriend, arrived at the murder house at about 10.10 the next morning, in his orange Metro. He was furious, and spoiling for a fight.

Although it was old news for the local radio station, Seawave, they still had a man there, Alan Proctor. He was leaning against his car in the shade, opposite No. 27, Tuebrook Road. Outside the house – a small, brick terrace with a deep maroon door and heavy curtains drawn at all the windows – was a policeman. He was in his shirtsleeves, and he was red with the heat. It was Terry Slater.

David parked his car behind Alan's, and locked it without thinking. A few Asian kids were kicking a ball about nearby, and there were some Asian men near the corner of the street. As you would expect in this area. Hindley Lane End. David hung his sports jacket over his shoulder, his notebook sticking from the left-hand pocket. He approached Alan Proctor, who raised a hand in greeting.

'Hi,' he said. 'Front line troops at last. Trust the *Echo* to be late.'

'What gives?' asked David. 'I heard your piece last night. Very good, I thought. What's the latest angle?'

'Oh,' said Proctor. 'Thanks. There isn't a lot more to it, actually, though. Straight.'

Great, thought David. Another one. He'd already had quite a run-in over this story. Almost a row with Sam Renton, the news-editor. He'd been treating it like a big one, something startling, and Renton had thought he was crazy.

'You what?' he'd said, disbelievingly. 'You're expecting it

to be the splash? It won't even make the front page unless you turn up something amazing, mate.'

'But it's a race murder,' said David, taken aback. 'The fascists on the rampage. It could be another –'

'Race murder my foot,' said Renton. 'It's some old gook who got his head bust in. They'll probably arrest his wife this afternoon.'

'The NF's big down there,' said David. 'All the Nazi nutters. How do you know it's domestic? It could –'

The phone on the newsdesk rang. Renton gave him a withering look and picked it up.

'Newsdesk. Renton. Yeah, hold.'

He clapped his hand over the mouthpiece and looked at David.

'Listen, flower,' he said. 'Stop fantasising and get down to Hindley Lane End. If you find the place crawling with blackshirts, jolly good. But you won't. It's a tin-pot head-bashing, all right? And we do *not* want to bore the pants off our readers with one dead Indian whose name the comps won't spell right. Got it?'

He did not wait for a response. He started speaking into the telephone, running his hand through his thick black hair. David left, grinding his teeth.

'Oh,' he said to Alan Proctor. 'Not a lot, you reckon. Is there *anything*!?'

'Sorry, Dave,' Proctor grinned. 'I'm not spinning you a line, honest. There's nothing new. Like I said on the air last night, old geezer called Yusuf Mansoor, head beaten to a pulp, found by a member of the family, his son I think. Mohammed, inevitably. I popped down on the offchance of something turning up, but it's dead.'

A police car turned into the street and drew up outside the house. David watched two men get out. PC Updike and PC Gardiner. Brian and Tony. He knew quite a few policemen, both from routine visits to HQ, and from going out with Sandra, although that, of course, was secret. But they were not friends.

Brian – tall, powerful and blond – nodded distantly.

Tony Gardiner, a small, wiry man, smiled. David made a gesture and Proctor waved.

'Right,' he said to David. 'I'm off. No point wasting my time round here. See you.'

As Proctor drove away, the roof of his car shimmering as it entered the harsh sunlight, David sauntered across the road. He was hardly angry any more. More depressed. The three policemen were standing around the front door, talking. They stopped as he approached.

'Hi,' he said. 'What's new?'

They looked at him evenly. He was shorter than all of them, and rather slightly built. He had black hair, quite long, and a drooping moustache. Terry shook his head.

'Nothing much,' he said. 'Just a simple murder, really.'

'I heard the NF might have had a hand,' said David. He told the lie quite calmly, as part of the game. It was sometimes possible to rattle them. But not today. The policemen glanced at each other, exchanging small smiles.

'No NF, chum,' said Brian. 'Just a 'orrible Asian bashes in another 'orrible Asian's 'ead. Get it?'

He and Tony Gardiner laughed. Terry smiled briefly, looking away.

David bit his lip.

'No signs of entry or anything, then?' he asked. 'Are you expecting to arrest anyone soon?'

The policemen's faces were blank.

'You know the rules, chum,' said Brian at last. 'You'll have to ask at the station, won't you? Don't try and get us into trouble, eh?'

There was tension creeping in. Terry coughed.

'It's pretty straightforward,' he said. 'Just a domestic. There's not a racial angle.'

'That's what they said about . . .' David stopped. He shrugged. No point in starting an argument. Just a glorious waste of time.

He started walking towards the orange Metro, pulling his keys out automatically. He unlocked the door and looked at the policemen, stark in the blazing sun. He blinked, his eyes recovering from the sudden gloom. They looked placidly back. Terry raised a hand in salute.

'They'll tell you everything you want to know back there,' he said. He sounded half apologetic. 'At HQ. Union Street. They'll see you right.'

David drove off.

When David had become a reporter on the *Echo*, Sandra – still at school – had expected to lose him. Instead of being glad about the terrific job, she's cried in his arms. David had been quite pleased, felt quite important; but he hadn't understood at all what she'd been crying about. When she'd said it was because he'd meet such interesting people, attractive girls, clever women, he'd laughed out loud.

'Sandra, Sandra,' he'd said. 'You can't be serious! Look at you. Look at me. You're incredible, the best-looking girl I've ever met. And I'm just a scrawn-pot. With spots. You're crazy.'

Her body had been beautiful, true enough. But David's was as well, to her. He was skinny, and had spots, but so what? She loved him. And he was clever.

Now, lying on the beach in the Saturday morning holiday crowd, Sandra opened her eyes, lifted her head, and stared at herself again. She grunted. Yeah, she was still all there, no question. She was brown, in a dazzling red bikini, and her legs were slim and shapely. Her body was all right. The trouble was, she wasn't too happy about her relationship any more. Or maybe just today. She was having a mood.

When Sandra had joined the police force, the fears of a break-up had started off anew. Not because *she'd* meet such interesting people, however – far from it! Some of David's crowd – his newspaper pals – didn't like the pigs, as they sometimes charmingly called them. Every now and then it led to friction.

Sandra, who had lain back on her towel once more, raised herself onto one elbow. She shaded her eyes and looked down the shingle at the sea, then across its sparkling, head-dotted surface, to the gaggle of sailing boats beyond. She felt very strange and angry.

'I don't know what's the matter with me,' she muttered.

She sat up and rubbed suntan cream into her thighs, morosely. The noise on the beach was terrific, but she was unaware. Hundreds, thousands, of holiday-makers, with their million kids. The traffic moving constantly along the promenade behind her, the screams and metallic music from the fairground on the pier. She wiped her hands on her towel and reached for her tin of lemonade. She pushed the curls off her face and swigged. She lay down and closed her eyes. She thought of David.

He wasn't spotty any more, and he'd put on lots of weight and muscle. He'd begun to dress well in the last year or so, and there was no denying it, he looked good. Maybe a few of his colleagues weren't all that nice, but David was, he was considerate and generous. Sandra couldn't understand her mood at all, there was just no cause for it. She felt like a row.

Impatiently, she sat up again, and shook her head. She saw David approaching, picking his way between the crowds of people, his shirt collar open, his jacket slung over his shoulder, moving towards their normal place beneath the Alhambra clock. In spite of herself, she gritted her teeth.

'Hi there, old girl,' he said. He dropped his coat on her bag and sat down, dragging at his shoes. 'God, it's stifling. Unbearable.'

In three minutes flat he was sitting beside her in his bright blue trunks on his bright gold towel. He raised his eyebrows, gave her a quizzing smile.

'Well,' he said. 'Aren't you pleased to see your very own Press baron?'

Sandra did her level best. She looked him in the eyes and smiled. It wasn't much, but it almost made her face hurt. She tried to say hello.

'I wish you wouldn't call me that,' she said. Her voice was thin and bitter. '"Old girl". It makes me ruddy mad.'

If David hadn't felt so drained and ragged himself, a fight might still have been avoided. But Sandra's words – and particularly her tone – cut straight into the knot of anger left inside him. He lost his cool, immediately. He attacked her with the most telling insult he knew.

'Chee, Sandra,' he said. 'You've never been the same, have you, since you joined the pigs? You've never been the same.'

If she was going to avoid a full-scale disaster, she had to keep calm. Her jaw ached. She said nothing. After a minute David carried on.

'I've had just about a bellyful today,' he said. 'Just about a gutful. First that swine Renton, then your racist mates in the force. That Brian lout, and PC Gardiner, and that fat smelly devil Slater. I don't know how you can work with them.'

He was breathing fast, but she was breathing faster. She closed her eyes and concentrated hard. It was absurd. It was quite ridiculous. She still said nothing.

'There's been a murder in Hindley Lane End,' he said. 'Did you know that? And according to our newseditor it's not worth a light. One dead Asian equals half a million bored readers. He *said* that to me, he *said* it.'

Sandra had heard the news that morning, on Seawave, in the bath. A Mr Mansoor, down Tuebrook Road. It hadn't sounded much.

'And your friends weren't any better,' said David. 'That Aryan charmer Brian Updike made it pretty plain what he thought. Some sort of joke. A cheap, pathetic joke. It's no wonder they call you pigs. You certainly behave like them.'

Sandra felt rage in the pit of her stomach. Her voice was strained and high.

'If people insist on calling us pigs I suppose some of us will always act the part,' she said.

'Neat,' he said. 'And I suppose if you insist on acting the part some of us will always call you pigs. Grunt. Grunt. Grunt.'

There was a pause. The breath hissed in their nostrils. Sandra was lying on her belly now, her head cradled on her arms, facing away from David. She wondered what she was doing there, what they expected of each other. She put the corner of her towel in her mouth and bit it. The sun was hot on her back, but there wasn't any pleasure in it. It was spoiled. David started to say something, then thought better of it. It came out as a grunt, half bitten off.

Sandra was angry, but there was sadness creeping in. His reaction had been violent, certainly, but she knew she'd started it. Now the mood was inexplicably seeping away. She listened to the background clamour and the cool, irregular crashing of the waves on the shingle. She was tired.

She heard David dressing, and she tried to look at him, to sit up and apologise for her part in the fiasco. She didn't make it.

Without another word, he walked off. The crunching of his feet was soon swamped by the other sounds.

THREE

That evening, luckily, David had to cover a Round Table charity dinner. Sandra sometimes went with him on these 'dos', but she often ducked out, because they could be rather boring. She used police work as her excuse normally, but tonight it was unnecessary. He didn't even bother to ring her.

In fact, she'd already arranged to go for a drink with Maggie. Roger, who was a keen model-builder – stockpiling for when his kids were old enough – had agreed to stay in baby-sitting. The two sisters took the car and went down to the Crown and Cushion, on the waterfront. It was a big, old pub that had been poshed up for the better class of person. Later on, it would become full of holiday-makers, but they got there early enough to get a good seat on the balcony, overlooking the harbour.

Maggie brought back two gin and tonics and they sat in silence for a while, watching the late sailing boats moving slowly through the harbour entrance against the tide. The sun was very low, but there was still only a small breeze, and it was warm and pleasant. The sisters were close, and it worried neither of them that they had nothing to say. They were quite contented.

After about an hour, when they'd had another gin and gossiped desultorily about Mum's bad leg and things, two men tried to chat them up. They were a little drunk and very jolly, with Midlands accents. The girls smiled vaguely, and refused their offers of gin, and shooed them away, but they were quite persistent. In the end Maggie flashed her wedding ring very meaningfully and told them bluntly to get lost.

When they'd gone she laughed, suddenly.

'When was it I was telling you I hadn't got chatted up for yonks?' she said. 'God makes liars of us all.'

After a while Sandra said: 'Mag, are all men like that? Don't they ever do anything except chat up? Can you have a man who's just a friend?'

'Well, I let you have driving lessons with Roger,' Maggie said. 'I sincerely hope you don't show your appreciation in the normal manner!'

Sandra glanced at her, a touch unsure. Maggie's small, bright face was sparkling with good humour.

'No seriously,' said Sandra. 'I often wonder. All the men I know are a bit like animals. No, I don't mean like that, I mean like wildcats. You know, sort of predatory. The way they look at you, and try to grab. They want to own you, to dominate.'

'What about David, then?' asked Maggie. 'He seems a nice enough bloke. I hardly see him as a predator.'

Sandra watched the pale blue ferry boat move across the harbour. Its steaming lights were on, although it was hardly even dusk. She found it very beautiful, carving a white track through the darkening waters. She thought for some time before answering.

'He patronises me,' she said. 'He tries to get away with murder. Oh, I know I'm being unfair, we had a fight today and it was me much more than him, I had a funny on. But he calls policemen pigs. And me. And expects me to laugh about it.'

'Whee,' said Maggie. 'The nasty little devil.'

Sandra lapsed into silence, toying with her glass. She felt that Dave *was* predatory, somehow, but she couldn't put it into words. And then again she was maybe being stupid. He was a nice bloke, kind and gentle. But his attitude, at times . . . The business of the police. He expected her to share his opinions. And then he called them pigs.

Maggie went and got more drinks.

'Do you love him, gal?' she said.

Sandra poured in half the bottle of tonic, and swilled the strong gin round her mouth. She adored it.

'I dunno anymore, Maggie. I honestly don't. I suppose so. But he can't half be a pain, I tell you.'

'Do you sleep with him?'

Sandra glanced at her sister, surprised.

'Course I do,' she said. 'You know that, don't you?'

Maggie grinned.

'Well not officially, love,' she said. 'I am your big sister. And Mum and Dad don't know, I'll bet.'

They both laughed then. But when they'd finished, Sandra said soberly: 'There's another problem, too. Dave can be so *jealous*. I think that's why he really hates the police. He thinks they're after me. All those great big hairy boys in blue. Hell, if only he knew!'

'What, those Flirty Fredericks? The hands-on-bottom brigade?'

'That kind of thing. He'd go hairless.'

A pause. They both still grinned from time to time.

Maggie: 'Are you ever tempted? I mean, do you ever . . . sort of . . . *like* it? You know.'

Sandra: 'Good God no. I –'

She broke off. She thought of Brian. It hadn't occurred to her before, but she was attracted, quite definitely attracted. He was a powerful man, with a powerful mind and hands. He was a divorcee and he was definitely predatory, definitely. But in some odd way he was exciting, he *could* get to her, deep down. She'd never really recognised it until now.

'Crikey, Mag,' she said, confused. 'I think I might. Heck. D'you know, I think I do.'

'Ah,' said Maggie. 'It's a devil, isn't it? It came as a real shock, that, to me as well.'

'What did?'

'When I discovered I fancied other blokes. Aside from Roger. I know just what you mean.'

Sandra felt she might be pushing her luck, but what the

hell? She asked: 'Have you ever done it? Been unfaithful? As they say.'

'Chance would be a fine thing, lover,' said Maggie. 'Two kids don't leave you a lot of time for that sort of thing. No, I haven't, actually.' She drank. 'And I do love Roger. No doubt in my mind, Sandra, none at all. But the thing is . . . I still see a bloke sometimes, not very often but sometimes, and I think . . . I think . . .'

After a minute or so Sandra, deeply curious, said: 'What?'

'Well I didn't want to be crude, my lovely,' said Maggie. 'So I stopped. But I sometimes think – I know – I wouldn't mind at all. Mm.'

They sat there for a long time more, and put their coats on when the evening chill came down. They chatted easily, about the family, kids, all sorts of things. They had a smashing night, the two of them, and Sandra went home tipsy. It was good.

Oddly enough, David and Sandra had a smashing day on Sunday, against all the odds. When he pulled up outside the semi where she lived with her parents, on an airy estate uptown, Sandra was still in bed. She hadn't even been sure he'd turn up. She lay there listening to the chat from downstairs, watching the curtains twitching in the breeze, making sunshine flashes across her pale cream bedroom wall. She took a long time in the bathroom, as long as she liked. It didn't matter leaving David with her Mum and Dad, they'd known him yonks and were comfortable.

She got a claustrophobic feeling as she washed and dressed, but she crushed it down. To be honest, she'd have rather David hadn't come after yesterday's mess-up, and she dreaded that another row would brew. But she felt quite guilty, also, at some of the things she'd admitted last night to her sister. And herself. She felt obscurely she ought to make up for them.

Unknown to her, of course, David was also bent on making up, and it brought out the best in both of them.

18

They went for a long drive in the Metro, over the hill and far away, they had a terrific lunch in a lovely little country pub they found, and they walked and slept it off in the lush warm countryside. At about tea-time they made love in a clearing in a wood and it was fabulous. Afterwards Sandra lay with her head on David's neck and said: 'I love you, Dave. I love you.'

And she meant it.

In a room at Union Street HQ, a slight, thin Asian boy stood against a bare white wall, weeping. His eyes were tightly closed and he was shaking in his knees and hands through lack of sleep. If he did not sleep soon, he thought, he would collapse. He cried silently, the tears pouring down his brown and haggard face. Out of the buzzing silence in his ears he heard a voice, boring and insistent.

'Right, Mohammed,' it said. 'Let's start all over, shall we? Let's take it from the top. And this time, laddie, let's make it true, eh? We've got all the time in the world, my little sunkissed sunshine, and there's nobody in the whole creation knows you're here. It's just us, sunshine, you and us. So how about it, Mohammed? Let's make the story true.'

FOUR

David was the office early-man on Monday. He parked the
Metro in his reserved place, said hello to the girls opening up
the front office, and climbed the wide curved staircase to the
newsroom. It was quite odd, deserted. A dozen desks, each
with a portable typewriter on it, ranged six to each wall. At
the top of the room, in front of a big wide window looking
out over the despatch yard, the newsdesk, long and
important-looking. It had four black telephones on it, and a
big pile of untouched newspapers. Also the diary, filing
trays, pens and pads.

Before he got down to work, David went and sat in Sam
Renton's chair, which was big and old, with a curved wood
back. In his mind's eye he saw the reporters, bent busily over
their desks, some typing, some on the phone, some making
notes. If he looked carefully, and cocked his head a little, he
could see Anne Higgins's legs. She had amazing legs, always
encased in sheer, shining, pale nylon. Lucky old Sam!

He got out of the newseditor's seat and moved to one on
the end of the desk, facing the pile of newspapers. He looked
at the clock. Eight-seven. He reached into a drawer, took
out the office transistor, and switched it on. It was already
tuned to Seawave, playing soft music for the early morning
masses. He turned it low. Luckily, they always signalled
their news-spots with a triple plangent chime. He'd not miss
it.

David didn't expect to find a reference to the Mansoor
murder in the populars, but he thought it might have made
the *Telegraph* or the *Guardian*. His job as early-man was to
scan the lot, though, so he started with the tabloids. He'd

20

finished flipping through them – finding nothing worthy of a local follow-up for when the reporters started rolling in – and was reaching for the *Telegraph*, when the radio gave its triple chime. A voice he recognised as Barbara Sherwood's wished the world good morning and started to read the local bulletin. He jotted down one or two items to refer to Sam, but it was all pretty dull. When she signed off it was a couple of bars into the next disc before he realised, with a start, that no mention had been made of the murder case. He shook his head. It was amazing.

At twenty to nine, when Sam came in, David had just put down the *Times*. Nothing, like the *Guardian* and the *Telegraph*. It was as if Mr Mansoor had never lived.

'I don't believe it, Sam,' he said, as Renton got his coat off. 'Not even Seawave mentioned it. The lovely sexy Sherwood didn't say a word. Incredible.'

Sam sat down and started on his morning ritual. He drew an unopened pack of Disque Bleu from his top right-hand desk drawer and opened it slowly and lovingly. Then he tapped one out with his finger nail, smelled it, put it into his mouth and lit it with a match from the same drawer, which he struck on the surface of the desk. He drew deeply on it, inhaled the smoke, then sat holding it in his lungs, leaning backwards, staring at the ceiling. Then he expelled it in two columns from his nostrils, sat upright, and sighed.

'Ah,' he said. 'That's good. That's very good. Now, what was that you said, flower?'

David rather scorned this ritual, but he knew better than to interrupt it. He said, with exactly the same emphasis, and in exactly the same tone: 'Not even Seawave mentioned it. I don't believe it, Sam. Incredible.'

'What, flower? What's incredible? What did the "lovely sexy Sherwood" fail to mention?' He changed his tone. 'I didn't know you fancied her as well,' he said. 'She's a cracker, isn't she?'

'The murder,' said David. 'The Mansoor job. No follow-up, no damn all. The police must have got somewhere with it, it's more than forty-eight hours.'

'Maybe there's nothing to say,' said Sam. He took another deep drag and scratched his thick black hair.

'Oh come on,' said Dave. 'Ruddy hell, Sam, if it'd been a white guy all hell would have broken loose. The town would be swarming with law. You know that.'

Sam, who had been holding the smoke deep down in his lungs, blew it slowly through his rounded lips. He stared hard at David.

'You're talking rubbish, you are,' he said. 'Do you know that, Dave? Pure, unadulterated rubbish.'

David, to his annoyance, felt himself go red.

'How do you mean?' he mumbled.

'You're obsessed, is what I mean,' Sam Renton said. He reached across and switched the radio off. 'The lovely Barbara didn't mention the Mansoor case because it is the pits. Zilch. Zero. You've got this weird idea that it's a racial thing. It's not. You went down there on Saturday, intent on standing it up. You didn't. It's a simple, straightforward, boring, murder.'

'If it *was* a racial thing,' David began.

'We'd follow it up,' said Renton. 'Just as long as it was a story. We're interested in stories, mate, and nothing else. Good, solid, stories. Got it?' He knocked the ash off his cigarette and coughed. 'Don't be a prat all your life, Dave,' he said, not unkindly. 'You're young. You haven't been at it all that long. You'll make a good reporter someday, sure. But you've still got some to learn. See?'

David felt miserably embarrassed. Sam was an easy-going guy, but it was quite a put-down. The door at the other end opened and three reporters came in, to start work. One was Anne Higgins. David cursed his blushing face.

'God,' said Renton. 'Is that the time? You'd better do the calls, Dave. And when you ring the fuzz, go easy on the Mansoor thing, right?' He smiled broadly. 'As an exercise in self-control!'

He reached for the diary and flipped it open. As he did so his phone rang. David lifted another phone and dialled the police. Nothing, they reported, on the Mansoor case.

Investigations under way, no arrests, no special angles. No. Lorry crashed on the hill, two hurt. A couple of other things.

When David put down the phone, Renton was waiting.

'Got your toothbrush in the car?' he said. 'That was Ted's wife. He's bumped, the lazy swine. Gastric flu or something. You'll have to go to Lewes, it's the Knox case. It'll be all week I should think.'

'I'd better nip home and get a suitcase packed,' said David. 'It's too long for the overnight bag.'

'Fair enough,' said Sam. 'But make it snappy. Ted should have been almost there by now, the case is due at ten. I'll ring Simons and get him to cover till you arrive, all right? And I'll get Julie to book you in at the Waverley. We'll need a story every lunchtime, early, and a full piece for overnight. Get it in by five-fifteen. Can do?'

'Yeah,' said David. 'Smashing. Hey, it's a great case, Sam. Terrific story.'

Sam Renton smiled.

'Sure is, flower,' he said. 'It's got everything. Poison, a mistress, wife's body in a burnt-out car, solid local angle. Everything.

'And,' he said, 'they're white. Every last one of them. Now that, young feller, is news.'

David left.

Down at headquarters, in Union Street, Sandra was being initiated into the mysteries of routine. She was in a small, stuffy office with two policewomen known as Jackie One and Jackie Two, and she was not enjoying herself. It was raining outside, with a curtain of water flowing gently down the window, obscuring the view, but it was not a cold day. All three of them were dressed in skirts and blouses only, but they were overhot and a little irritable.

In front of them, on a large varnished table, were the beginnings of the Mansoor case filing system. Three piles of neat, unmarked cards, two untidy piles of cards with names and details on, and a sheaf of typewritten reports that Jackie

One and Jackie Two were laboriously wading through. Every few minutes one or other of them would call for a card and Sandra would pick it up and hand it to them. The cards were well within their reach, of course, but this was her task. She was the junior, learning the job. Whenever a card was full, Jackie One or Jackie Two would hold it up to Sandra, and indicate which pile it was for. She would take it, and put it on.

'You might make it a bit neater,' said Jackie Two acidly, after Sandra had dropped a card onto one of the untidy piles. 'Sloppiness doesn't help, you know. Care and neatness are the essence of police work.'

Sandra felt like telling her what to do with the card but she kept her cool. She didn't like Jackie Two and they tended to rub each other the wrong way. Jackie Two was only about twenty five and she'd been the HQ beauty before Sandra arrived. Probably she was jealous. Or maybe, Sandra thought, she was just a sour-faced old boot.

'Yes,' said Jackie One, mildly. 'Keep 'em tidy, Sandy. It might be mindless, but it's better if you do it right.'

Jackie One was a much different proposition, and Sandra smiled at her and tidied up the piles. She was in her early forties, with a placid nature and tight dark curls streaked with grey. Although she'd been a policewoman for more than twenty years she'd picked up none of the mannerisms that got up people's noses. She was relaxed, and approachable, and humorous. She was still a constable and always would be.

'I suppose this just strikes you as a waste of time,' said Jackie Two, nastily. 'I suppose you think you should be out on patrol with some handsome young copper, gadding around the town.'

'On a day like this she'd have to be mad,' said Jackie One. 'Here, give us that card back will you, love? I think I got that last name wrong.'

Sandra gave Jackie One the card, and she checked it against the typed sheet.

'Right,' she said. 'I thought I'd mixed it up.'

'What I *don't* understand,' said Sandra, carefully, 'is why we've got to do these family trees and things when they've already got the bloke. I mean, that does seem peculiar.'

Jackie Two sniffed.

'Fat lot you know then,' she said.

When it became clear she was not going to add to that, Jackie One took over.

'Until they're sure, love,' she said. 'We've got to carry on. I mean, it's ninety nine per cent certain that this young feller did it, but we'd look daft if he didn't, wouldn't we? And we hadn't even made a start.'

Quite unconsciously, they'd all stopped working while they talked. Jackie Two went over to her jacket and lit herself a fag. She offered Jackie One the packet and she took one. They sat heavily down in chairs.

'I could kill a cuppa tea,' said Jackie One. 'Will you get us, Sandy?'

As they drank they filled her in on details. While the lads were out interviewing, and searching, and generally trying to stand up a case, the girls' job was to build up an accurate picture of the lives and relationships of everyone involved. Yusuf Mansoor, the murdered man; Mohammed, his son and murderer; the other children, much too young to bother with. All the neighbours – mostly Asian – all the relatives, all the friends. They had to be identified, given a card, cross-referenced. It was a long job, and painstaking, and pretty boring at that. But it was absolutely vital.

'All that stuff on telly's rubbish, see,' said Jackie Two. 'Couple of sexy brilliant detectives mucking about in cars all night and the job's done. Quick shoot-out to keep the viewers happy and it's all over. Load of cods.'

Jackie One nodded.

'Nearly every successful enquiry comes down to one thing,' she told Sandra. 'Routine. Between us I bet me and Jackie have solved more crime than anyone else in town. Honest. You'd be amazed what can come out of writing people's names and details down.'

'Yeah,' said Jackie Two. 'And what thanks do we get? Damn all.'

Sandra waited for a polite interval to show she appreciated the injustices they suffered from, then asked: 'Why are they so sure it was the son? Have they said?'

Jackie Two said triumphantly: 'Because he found the body. It's the biggest giveaway of all. If you find the body, you've put it there. A golden rule.'

According to Jackie One it was true. Most murderers thought it was a brilliant ploy – and it solved the problem of hiding the corpse, of course – but it was as old as crime. Pick up the one that found the body, and you'd usually got the villain.

'Course, a confession would be best,' said Jackie Two. 'According to the lads, though, this little git's as tough as nails. Only a weedy little thing he is, but he *will* not crack.'

The older woman shivered slightly.

'He's been down there now for ages, an'all. Be three days soon. He must be close to breaking point. I don't like the way they let that Sergeant Winter in on it. I don't think he's fair. He hates the blacks. He's NF, they reckon.'

Jackie Two snorted.

'You're getting soft,' she said. 'They've got to break him, haven't they? He's a murderer, isn't he? Couple more days without sleep, with Ted Winter and Inspector Lyons on him, and he'll see sense all right. He'll confess to anything.'

'Without sleep?' said Sandra, shocked. 'How do you mean?'

Jackie One glanced at Jackie Two, and Jackie Two looked slightly shifty.

'Not literally, love,' said Jackie One. 'It's only in a manner of speaking, like. But Jackie's right. You can't treat them like the best teaset, can you? He may be only a little weed, but you should have seen his old man's bonce. I saw a couple of the pictures. Like a bowl of pink blancmange, it was.' She stubbed her fag. 'Listen,' she said. 'We'd better get on. We haven't got all day.'

They had, of course, and for the next hour they worked

solidly at their cards. By lunchtime Sandra was almost mad with boredom, she felt exhausted. It was raining hard, but she went out for a walk, to clear away a slight headache. There was, however, better news when she rejoined the Jackies in their room.

'They're setting up a caravan tomorrow,' said Jackie Two. 'The quicker we can get this stuff out of the way, the more chance we've got of going down. That'd be much more fun.'

The caravan was an incidents room. It would be towed to Hindley Lane End and smothered with information posters, in lots of Asian languages. The idea was that a couple of officers could man it through the day, and take down information as people came in. They were going to get an interpreter as well, from the university down the coast.

Although they'd been over the ground before, Sandra had to ask. This sounded an even more bizarre waste of time and money than the family trees.

'But why?' she said. 'When we've got him in the cells? Wouldn't it at least be better to wait a day or two in case he does confess?'

Jackie Two looked at her with a sneer.

'We can't wait, stupid,' she said. 'He's a Pakistani. If we don't do something soon we'll have the do-gooders on our necks. The race relations lot. Mr Kenny Baby Shaw, the black man's friend. He's a troublemaker.'

Sandra looked to Jackie One for an opinion. She half-nodded.

'You can't be too careful, love,' she said: 'You know how these things snowball. There's the Press to think of. They love to knock the police, they can't get enough of it.'

Sandra opened her mouth to protest, and David popped into her mind. She bit his name off, made a sort of cough. To be linked with the Press would be stupid, utterly insane. And in any case – well . . . they could be right, in a way. He certainly had this thing about the force.

'It just needs Kenny Baby to stick his nose in, then that black Commie mate of his, Rastus or whatever, and we're in the slime,' said Jackie Two. 'The Press would go bananas. The caravan'll take the wind right out of their sails. Brilliant.'

Sandra coughed again.

'Frog,' she said. 'In the throat. I'll go and get a . . . anyone else want one? I'll go and get some coffee . . .'

FIVE

Over the next few days, Sandra spent many hours in the incidents caravan. It was a weird, bruising time of boredom, worry and confusion. And at the end of the third day she agreed to go out with Brian.

She was first driven down to the van – by Brian – the next afternoon. She'd spent another unpleasant morning with Jackie Two sorting out the Mansoor files, and the relief of getting away was almost physical. Jackie One had been sent off in the morning, to set the paperwork in the van up, so they had been alone together, and the friction had been obvious.

Jackie Two, suspecting that Sandra was having problems with the racial aspects of the case, had really piled it on. She'd bitched and binded incessantly about how the 'wogs' were getting preferential treatment, and how it was a crying shame. She told horror stories of how you had to bend over backwards to be nice to them, how they got kid-gloves treatment, how you got the sack if you didn't treat them like visiting royalty. Sandra knew it was utter rubbish, atrocious nonsense – and maliciously aimed at her – but she had to take it. Rule One: Don't argue with a superior.

'This caravan thing's a case in point,' said Jackie Two. 'Why the hell should *we* go to *them*? It's sickening. If they were normal human beings and they had some evidence or anything, they'd come to the station, or stop someone on the beat or something. But no, we've got to go crawling down to them. It's costing pounds, thousands, it must be. What do you say?'

Sandra smiled vaguely, and mumbled. She didn't want

to say anything. But she wouldn't get away with that.

'Yeah,' she said. 'Yeah, it does seem a bit daft.'

It did, as well, and the evening before she'd pondered long about what she really felt about the whole affair. She wondered if the murder boy had really been kept without sleep, and if Ted Winter really was a member of the Front. She was entirely used to casual racism from her colleagues in the force – and many other people as well – but she didn't take it seriously. To hear Brian, or Tony Gardiner, or even her Dad, talk about 'wogs' and 'jungle-bunnies' and 'Pakis' didn't worry her that much. She knew it didn't mean a lot. Her father was a kindly man, who even had some coloured mates at work. He was on the buses, an inspector. He talked like that, at home, or to his friends, but he had no hatred in him, none at all.

She'd decided in the end that the Jackies' stories were something like her Mum's. Before her leg got bad, her Mum had been a nurse. She had a fund of hospital horror tales that would make your hair stand on end, it was a wonder anyone ever survived, even as an outpatient. For years, Sandra had thought they were true, and her Mum, as far as you could tell, always had, however crazy they might be. But it was a mythology, a sort of private language of the trade. Over the years Sandra had met other nurses – including school friends who'd gone into it – and they'd told the same sort of tales. The very *same* tales, in fact, in many cases. And believed them, told them as actual fact. Sandra had been comforted. If Sergeant Winter was a fascist, she'd eat her hat. And she suspected, strongly, that an incidents caravan was perfectly normal in a case like this – whether the victim was black, white or sky-blue pink.

The days in the caravan soon began to shake her, though. The weather had gone back dry once more, and it was vaguely thundery, which didn't help a lot. Even with just the police inside, the van was overcrowded, and smelly, and blisteringly hot. Sitting, they were all jammed up together, with their legs touching and sticking. Standing, trying to walk about, it was a case of bumping into each other, and squeezing uncomfortably past in the formica passageways. It would have been paradise for a Flirty Frederick, but the sergeant and the constable on the job were not like that, and they were in any case bad-tempered and preoccupied, while the interpreter merely looked deeply uncomfortable and unhappy. He was white.

Brian, on the drive down to Hindley Lane End, had chatted Sandra up in a routine way, and ended with the standard request that she come out for a drink. She'd refused, thanking him prettily, and he'd asked her if she'd still got a boyfriend. It was not a new question, by any means, but Sandra surprised them both with her answer.

'No,' she'd said. 'I haven't.'

She was standing at the open door of the Panda, looking in. Her hand was on the handle.

Brian grinned.

'Hey!' he said. 'That's new, beautiful. When did that happen? Does that mean –'

She slammed the door and spoke through the window.

'It means nothing,' she said. 'Absolutely nothing. You're on duty. So am I.'

And she ran into the caravan, leaving Brian sitting there. He waited for several seconds before he drove away.

Despite what Jackie One and Jackie Two had said, the caravan looked like being as boring as the family trees. It emerged almost instantaneously that she had been sent there to organise the kitchen, presumably because Jackie One had either refused or had been genuinely too busy sorting out the paperwork. When she'd stepped inside there had been a universal cry of relief, and within two minutes she was standing at the tiny sink, washing up the mugs while the kettle boiled on the Calor ring.

Afterwards she was given other things to do, but it was on the same level as before – handing papers, opening drawers, sharpening pencils and so on. Most of the time she was just there, apparently, to watch.

At first, there wasn't much to see. She'd arrived towards the end of lunchtime, and Jackie One had said things had

31

been quite slack. But by mid-afternoon there were about seven people queuing in the van, waiting to be seen, and another ten or a dozen outside.

It was very odd and not very pleasant. All the people who had come were Asians, and they were clearly very poor. There was a lot of unemployment in the town and they looked somehow tatty, and downtrodden. The men ranged from pale brown to quite dark, and there were none under about forty five. There were far fewer women, dressed in Eastern clothes.

Despite the posters plastered on the van, there was obviously a lot of confusion in many minds as to what it was there for. Some of the people, it soon turned out, had nothing to say about the murder, and almost all of them were clutching passports. For some incomprehensible reason they insisted on showing them, thrusting them under the policemen's faces. There were many misunderstandings, and at one point the sergeant, exasperated to the point of fury, seized a passport from a tiny, ancient man, and hurled it to the floor. His face had gone dark with rage and he suddenly stood up, towering above the little Indian.

He opened his mouth as if to shout, but in the event said nothing. He merely stood there, flexing his large, pink hands, his lips working. After a few moments the Asian bent humbly, and picked up his passport. He looked up at the huge, angry policeman and gave a tiny bow. Then he shuffled out.

That evening, Sandra had stayed at home, tired and preoccupied. Her Dad, whose senses were very finely tuned where she was concerned, had asked her what was up. She'd smiled, and told him the thundery weather and her work. But she wouldn't go into details. Just said she was in the caravan by the docks, and it was hot, and heavy, and nasty. David rang from Lewes, absolutely full of himself, but she listened only listlessly to the details of the court case. She went to bed early and unhappy, and slept like a log.

In the next couple of days she learned about reality from the outside in and the inside out. It was an utterly exhausting time. She felt quite drained. The shuffling line of silent, watchful Asians marched through her dreams. Even in the caravan she sometimes twitched, suddenly awakened from a sleep or coma, she never knew quite which.

The confusions seemed to grow rather than diminish. More documents appeared, festoons of passports were shoved under their noses. The nerves of all of them got raggeder and raggeder, blow-ups got more frequent. Sandra, despite herself, unconsciously, grew to hate the shuffling lines. They seemed so stupid, so utterly without hope.

The language thing was awful. Although the interpreter sounded fluent to an English ear, he obviously did not to many of the Asians. He offered Hindi, Urdu and Gujerati, apparently in that order. Some people shook their heads when he had spoken, totally puzzled. Then people behind would join in, helping out. Soon there would be an absolute babble of Asian tongues and the police would sit there helpless, alone and lost. Until the sergeant would swell with rage and frustration and roar and hammer till he got them silent.

'It's like a bear-garden,' he said, during a long tea-break when they'd put the shutters up to keep them out. 'It's like a lunatic asylum. It's like going down to Bedlam.'

He had a mug of coffee in his hand, and his hand was shaking with exhaustion. His face was grey. The constable beside him, sweating profusely in the heat and smelling strong, was more inclined to rage.

'It's impossible,' he hissed. 'Impossible, impossible. They're doing it on purpose, they must be. It's impossible.'

Jackie One said: 'It's the passports that get me. Why the passports? Do you know, not *one* of them has turned up without a passport.'

The interpreter, who had been somehow shrinking in upon himself as the days dragged by, somehow getting smaller in discomfort and embarrassment, said quietly: 'You can hardly blame them. The way the Government goes on. They think . . . they must believe . . .'

Three pairs of hostiles eyes regarded him. Sandra stared

33

at the floor, but she felt a flash of rage herself. Was he *defending* them?

'Great,' said the constable. 'So it's the Government's fault now, is it? And what about that one with her rent book, then? What about that daft cow? They're *thick* mate. They're a rabble. They're a . . . They're a . . . Ach, to hell.'

The strange thing, Sandra found, was that even as she felt herself becoming more ragged, more prone to bursts of hate and fury, she could remember how she'd felt to start with. There'd been nothing racial about *her* discomfort. But by Thursday, she was prepared, with the rest of them except the interpreter, to blame everything including the heat on the Asians. She did not join her colleagues actively, perhaps, but her heart was with them, and they knew it. The interpreter had become an outcast; tolerated but ignored, rather like an unloved dog.

When Brian dropped by the caravan just as she was knocking off on Thursday, she was just about knackered. She walked towards the bus-stop with her head down, miserable and exhausted. She jumped when he appeared before her, and looked up, startled. He was dressed in civvies, grey trousers and a casual shirt.

He smiled broadly. He was handsome and relaxed.

'You look like a girl who needs a lift,' he said. 'May I escort you to my limousine?'

Sandra didn't try to argue. Nor did she when he invited her for a drink. She just nodded, dumbly, not managing a smile. She could do with a drink. She could *kill* a drink. She didn't even smile when she saw his car, a smart Opel with a personalised number plate. Normally, she'd have thought it as pseud as hell. Now it seemed all right, quite normal.

Brian drove fast and well, although he enjoyed going round corners a little too swiftly for Sandra's comfort. He liked the sound of squealing rubber. They went north through the city, over the hill and into the empty countryside beyond. The sun was still hot and high, and the windows were open wide. Sandra tore her tie off and threw it in the back with her hat. Slowly, she relaxed.

They pulled up outside a tiny, ancient pub beside a village green and Sandra, making herself look even less police by nipping into the ladies and tearing off her tights, sat on a rustic bench beside a duck pond. Brian brought her out a Pimms as a surprise and she drank it with delight, nibbling lazily at the trimmings. He drank a pint of bitter and she watched his Adam's apple bob. She felt better now, tired but happy. They still had hardly spoken.

When they did, it was Sandra's instinct to talk about the case, the caravan, because her mind was full of it. But Brian shushed her up.

'Don't talk police work,' he said. 'You've had a gutful. Relax. Forget it. It won't do any good. You're starting to learn, that's all. It's not a bed of roses.'

Wow, thought Sandra, you can say that again.

'What shall we talk about, though?' she said. 'It's all I can think about, Brian. My head's full of it. It's driving me up the wall.'

'Yeah,' he said. 'It's hard at first. Let's just talk about the ducks. Look at that one, there, the feller with the wrinkled beak. We should have brought some bread. We will do, next time.'

In the event, Brian did most of the talking. He talked about his childhood, and where he was brought up, and his marriage that had ended in divorce. He talked about the pressure of police work, and the fact that he had two children whom he was hardly allowed to see. He talked about a friend who'd emigrated, and how he felt a little lonely sometimes now, now that Terry had got his oppo, Tony Gardiner, back full-time after a recent secondment.

Sandra sat and watched and listened, hovering on the edge of sleepy trance. It was so relaxing, so unexpected. She looked at his strong handsome face, his large expressive hands and bare, hairy forearms, and listened to his pleasant, thoughtful voice. This was Brian Updike, she thought, the scourge of criminals and a demon hunter of the skirt. She felt utterly languid and content.

After another couple of drinks, Brian looked at his watch.

'You must be starving,' he said. 'Sorry about all the wittering. I'll take you home.'

She didn't argue, although she thought she'd rather eat with him. But her mother might be worried, she was already very late. She watched him out of the corner of her eye as he drove back to town, and once he glanced at her and smiled. Her stomach lurched. She felt elated. And afraid.

He dropped her at the end of her road, a good long way from home as instructed. He didn't try to kiss her, even. Just dropped his hand lightly on her knee, over her skirt.

'That was great,' he said, smiling. 'Lovely. Thanks, Sandra. Thanks a lot.'

She blushed, and stammered when she said goodbye. He smiled ironically, and she grabbed her hat and tie and ran.

Her mother was watching television when she went in, with her leg up on a pile of cushions.

'Hello, love,' she said. 'There's a salad out the back. Why don't you get yourself some milk from the fridge? You look all hot and bothered.'

Yeah, thought Sandra. Well!

SIX

David rang Sandra at eight o'clock on Friday night, after driving back from Lewes. The case had been a great one, and he knew he'd covered it well. He felt terrific.

'Hi,' she said. Her voice was flat.

'Hello, old girl,' said David. 'The famous newshound returns. Let me take you to the Kasbah and fill you up with a thousand and one Arabian delights. Including sherbet, of course. Or even gin and tonic.'

'No,' said Sandra. 'Sorry, Dave, I'm not coming out. I'll ring you tomorrow. Are you at work?'

'In the morning I am,' said David. 'Heh, what's up, old love, you sound tired.'

'I am tired,' said Sandra. 'I've been working all week, remember?'

'Pah,' said David. 'You call that work? You're always moaning they treat you like a teagirl. *I've* been in court all week, taking millions of words and filing two stories a day. And *I'm* not complaining.'

If Sandra had not been so exhausted, she would have become angry. It was an old dispute, although he'd said it jokingly.

'I'm not arguing,' she said. 'I'm just not coming out.'

At his end of the line, David rolled his eyes.

'Ah well,' he said, biting down a snide remark. 'Ah well, tomorrow then. All right?'

'I expect so,' said Sandra. 'I'm helping Dad in the garden all day, I promised. But I'll be clear in the evening.'

'Big night out,' said David. 'Celebration. One murderer down for life and his mistress for eleven years. Ought to bring a little comfort to your stony copper's heart. I'll take you for a meal. Suit?'

'Lovely,' said Sandra. She yawned. 'Yes, fine, Dave. What time, seven, seven thirty?' She yawned again.

'Gawd, you're a real ball of fire, you are,' said David. 'You'd better go to bed and recover from your oh-so-difficult week. Don't sleep with anyone I wouldn't sleep with.'

'What time?'

'Oh, make it seven thirty.' He'd been going to suggest a drive in the country, perhaps a wander in the woods. But he couldn't be bothered. Women.

They got off on a better footing the next evening, largely because Sandra had recovered. She'd had a proper lazy day with her Dad, rooting gently through the little garden while Mum sat on a long cane chair reading magazines and watching them. No one had said a lot, there wasn't much to say. It was the tonic she needed.

Just once they skirted close to talking seriously. It was her father's fine tuning at work. He was a kindly man, immensely fond of her.

'How you finding it in the force, then?' he asked casually, as they stood watching the smoking bonfire by the back fence. 'Still like it, do you?'

It had caused a stir in the family, her joining up. No one there was anti, or anything like that, but it had seemed rather an odd thing to do. Maggie had been particularly surprised.

'Why the fuzz?' she'd said. 'I didn't know you were the military type, gal. You're not into whips and boots, I hope!'

'Maybe it runs in the family, deep down,' her father had said. 'Bill wanted to join the Army, remember? Although I doubt if he'd of been a Redcap.'

Bill had been the oldest child. He'd been killed in a car crash on the hill when he was Sandra's age. He would have been nearly thirty now, if he'd lived.

Sandra, young and not too sure of herself, had blushed. She'd mumbled something about someone having to do it. Wanting to do her bit. She couldn't put it into words, exactly, but she did feel it. She admired the police, she thought them brave and honourable. And she thought it must be an extremely difficult job. That appealed to her most of all. She wanted something hard.

'They're not exactly popular these days,' Maggie had gone on. 'You'll get a lot of stick, gal. From your friends.'

Their Mum had snorted. Maggie, to her, was a waster. Working in an office for a lot of money until she'd married young. Mum believed in slogging. She'd been a nurse for years, and loved it.

'You leave her be,' she'd said. 'I reckon it's a jolly good thing. Do some real work. Some useful work. I think it's a jolly good idea, Sandra.'

Now, watching the acrid blue smoke climb into the clouded sky, Sandra pondered her father's question. But not for long.

'Oh yes, Dad. I still like it, 'course I do. I'm just knackered by it, that's all. It's been a heavy week.'

'Your first murder,' he said, mock humorously. 'I hope you don't make a habit of it, gal! They wear you out, I reckon.'

'Yeah. Well it's a strain, Dad, I won't deny it. In that caravan. All those Asians who can't speak a word of English. It's a strain.'

'It's a funny old world,' mused her father. 'Poor old sod. I saw the poster. He was properly knocked about, the little you could see. Blood everywhere. I wonder if he wished he'd stayed in India . . .'

Sandra thought about the nastiness of it all, her worries about Ted Winter, and long interrogations, and her own feelings of hate and shame in the reeking caravan. It left a bitter taste, all of it. It had been a rotten week, a cow. She said nothing.

Her father said, obscurely: 'Ah well, Sandy love, you'll do what's best, I know you will.' He poked the bonfire with a stick. He smiled at her. 'There's no doubt in my mind on *that* score, anyhow.'

The column of smoke moved towards them on the wind and enveloped them. They coughed, and moved away. They had a cup of tea with mother.

The first part of the meal was grand. They went to the Shalimar, and David ordered for both of them, with Sandra's permission. He'd been doing a bit of research, he said, in a smashing restaurant in Lewes, and he'd picked up a lot of tips. He smiled broadly, in a strangely intimate way, to the waiter, a small, dark man with a moustache and bright eyes, and said something to him that Sandra didn't catch, that sounded foreign. The waiter, startled, didn't reply. He left the menus and returned to the counter and till. David chuckled.

'That threw him,' he said. 'I gave him the Muslim greeting. *Salaamu eleicum.* If he hadn't been so surprised he'd have replied. *O eleicum salaam.*'

Sandra was glad he hadn't, but she regarded David affectionately. He didn't know how embarrassing he could be sometimes, but there wasn't any harm done. The waiter had probably just written him down as a nut. She didn't care tonight; she was happy.

'It's nice to see you, Dave,' she said. 'I take it you've had a lovely time.'

He launched into a long, and very funny, account of the court case, breaking off only to discuss the items on the menu in detail with the waiter. It had been real Agatha Christie stuff, no doubt of it, and the main 'villain' was a local businessman, being tried in Lewes because he was too well-known for a trial in the city court to be a fair one. There'd been arsenic, a burnt-out car over the Channel cliffs, a chase across half the South Coast, love-trysts in a Bristol flat – the lot.

They ate as they talked, so the tale went on for ages. Sandra was required only to nod and giggle from time to time, and she was enjoying her lamb bhuna a lot. She regretted slightly that David allowed his voice to get rather loud when he realised that people at other tables were listening to his story, but she didn't mind that much. She'd always known he had show-off tendencies, so she couldn't complain, she thought. Anyway, he was a bit tipsy and no one seemed to care. They were actually laughing.

When he'd run down, they ate in silence for a time. David smiled across the table and said, more quietly: 'You're looking great tonight, Sandra, I love that dress. Have you had a good week?'

She nodded.

'All right,' she said. 'You know. Nothing like as exciting as your murder, the one I've been working on. A real drag, actually.'

He was surprised.

'A murder? Have you been working on a murder? You didn't tell me.'

She hadn't. He'd been odd about the Mansoor thing, then she'd become too tired by it to risk bringing it up. Safer to keep her mouth shut. She nodded.

'Yes,' she said. 'Nothing to tell. It's just routine, that's all. A slog.'

David glanced round. The waiter was quite near but he appeared to deliberately raise his voice.

'I suppose you mean the Mansoor case,' he said. 'I wouldn't call it a slog. Nothing's happened since the day they found the body, has it? You're not going to tell me the police are actually trying, surely?'

Sandra felt herself colouring. She said levelly: 'David, this is not a performance, you know. We can't discuss it here.'

'Ach, you make me sick,' he said. His voice had taken a bitter edge, it was amazingly sudden. But he did speak lower. Sandra had fixed him with a really warning eye.

'Let's drop the subject, Dave,' she said. 'Please. I'm having a lovely time, I'm enjoying myself. Don't spoil it, love. I don't want to talk about it, in any case. I've had a really shitty week, if you must know. I don't want to talk about it.'

David's face had darkened, but it changed as the waiter approached the table.

'Was the meal all right?' he asked. 'Anything else now? Tea, coffee?'

David put on an expression that disturbed Sandra. She thought he must be drunk. He was being somehow over-friendly, smarmy even, with the waiter.

'Have you any rasmallai?' he asked. He glanced at Sandra. 'You'll love this,' he said. 'It's absolutely *wonderful*, old thing. Miraculous.'

They hadn't, and Sandra was glad. She could feel a disaster coming on, and she wanted out. She refused a tea or coffee and made it plain that she wanted to go. David paid up almost regretfully, and salaamed to the waiter at the door. This time the man returned the salute, with a smile that was mocking, Sandra thought. David was cockahoop, and she had to fight herself not to make a nasty crack.

They went to the Crown and Cushion, on the harbour-side, and it was full to bursting, and very noisy. The row was contained, but all the pleasantness was draining from the evening rapidly. David was drunk and sniping now, and she wondered how much longer she could take it.

'You see what I mean, though,' he said, insistently. 'If it had been a white that was killed they'd have pulled out all the stops, you know it. They just don't care, you *know*. Why can't you admit it?'

'Rubbish,' she snapped. 'What about that case in Birmingham a few months back? The gang of black thugs that set on that old white man and killed him? They never arrested anyone, did they? Well, *did* they?'

'Don't be so bloody naïve,' said David. 'That's different. It was in a huge open space, at night. Even the fuzz couldn't arrest every black in Birmingham and charge them all with murder, however much they'd like to. Be reasonable.'

Reasonable! She bit her lip.

'I'll bet you good money, Sandra,' he said, 'that that

caravan effort'll achieve nothing. It's PR, that's all. Public relations, to make sure no one can point the finger at them. They'll have a few coppers down there for a week or two, doing bugger all, then they'll pull out. Sorry, no clues. Sorry, no chance. Sorry.'

'Bugger all?' said Sandra. She saw a man beside them in the crush listening, looking curiously at her angry face. 'Bugger all?' she hissed, turning away from him. 'If only you knew. It's killing work, it's awful. You say we're not trying, and I'm practically dead from exhaustion, let alone the others. *Hours* of misery, *hours* of filing and cross-checking and paperwork. Look, I'm going!'

She slammed down her glass and began to push her way out, towards the car park. David swallowed his last mouthfuls of beer hurriedly and followed her. He caught up at the Metro. She was holding the door handle tightly, leaning on the roof, breathing the cool sea air rapidly and deeply.

'Bear up, old thing,' he said insultingly. 'You're in the pig force now. You must expect to get some aggro, you know.'

She did not speak. You patronising little bastard, she thought. You patronising little sod.

'I'll have a little bet with you,' he said. 'I'll bet you a week's wages they never nail anyone for this. I bet there's never even an arrest.'

'Never an arrest?' said Sandra, despite herself. 'What are you talking about, you fool? They picked up someone on the night. His son, Mohammed. What the hell are you on about?'

There was silence between them. David stared at her, swaying slightly. When he spoke at last, he spoke quietly.

'Are you pulling my leg?' he said. 'Are you telling me they're holding someone? For the Mansoor job?'

Sandra did not speak. She realised there *was* something wrong, something funny going on, and she knew she'd kept her mouth shut to David deliberately. David knew the ropes. He wouldn't be mistaken. She'd spoken out of turn. She'd blown the gaffe. Without even knowing how.

'Well,' said David, finally. 'Well, well, well. Now that *is* a story, Miss. That really *is* a story!'

'David?' she started. 'Dave . . .?'

Then she stopped. Oh Christ, just what was going on? What the hell was going on? She turned away.

'I'm going home by bus,' she said. 'You're a nasty little sod and I hate your guts. And if you drop me in it, David Tanner, I'll bloody kill you. And that's a bloody promise.'

She heard the door slam as she walked away.

SEVEN

Next day Sandra got up late, feeling terrible. She hadn't slept very well, inevitably, and finally she had not even known whether she was dreaming or thinking some of the things that were crowding into her head. It came as a relief when she heard the telephone ring, followed by her father's voice up the stairs that it was for her.

He did not say so, but she guessed it was David. She got out of bed and pulled her nightdress down, but did not bother with a dressing gown. The door between the hall and the kitchen was open, and both her parents were sitting at the table, also in night clothes. She smiled at them embarrassedly, but pulled the door closed nonetheless. This was not going to be easy.

She picked up the receiver.

'Hi,' she said.

David sounded nervous, as well he might.

'Hello, Sandra,' he said. 'Look, I'm sorry about last night.'

'So am I,' she said. 'I've had just about enough of it, in fact. And of you.'

There was a pause.

'Look,' he said. 'We've got to talk. It's urgent.'

'Well we can't,' said Sandra. 'I'm going to the country with my Mum and Dad. It's all arranged.'

'But it's raining. You'll get soaked.'

Sandra glanced at the frosted glass front door, then into the living room and through the window there. Hell. So it was. She carried on lying.

'Dad's borrowed a car. We're going away. We're going to my auntie's.'

'Damn, damn, damn, damn, damn,' said David. 'Can't you put it off, love? This is urgent.'

She didn't know what he was on about. What was so urgent about a row?

'You should have thought of that before you started it,' she said. 'I'll see you in the week, maybe. When I've thought about it.'

'Look old – Look, Sandra,' said David. 'It's not just the row. That was bad enough I admit, and I'm sorry, very sorry. But the other thing. The Mansoor thing. Look, we've got to talk about it. Now.'

She closed her eyes in weariness. So that was it. He hadn't phoned up to apologise, he was after information. She might have known.

'You heard what I said yesterday,' she said. 'And I meant it. If you take that any further, Dave, we're finished. Just no question any more. I've had enough.'

'But Sandra. You don't understand. It's fact, love. If it's true it's important. It's . . . Well, if what you said is right, it's illegal, apart from anything else. They can't do it. Not even the police.'

'If it's true,' said Sandra, desperately. 'If it's true. Well that's your problem, isn't it? You're the newshound. If it's true is for you to find out. I know nothing and I'm saying nothing, and if you stick your bloody nose in we're finished. I –'

She stopped, and pulled the receiver from her ear. She looked at it, shaking her head from side to side. She said 'Oh God' quietly, to herself.

As David's voice buzzed out of the receiver she shook her head once more, and put it down.

As she tried to get back up the stairs the kitchen door opened. Her father stood there in his striped pyjamas.

'What was that all about, Sandra?' he said. 'There's a cuppa here, gal.'

She followed him into the kitchen and sat at the formica table. Her mother poured her out a cup of tea.

'He's a nice boy, that David,' she said. 'I hope you're not having trouble with him, darling.'

Sandra smiled ruefully, and took a sip of tea.

'No,' she said. 'No trouble. He's just a fink, that's all. If he rings up again, Dad, tell him to jump in the harbour, will you? I've had a bellyful.'

David did ring back. about twenty minutes later. Sandra was at the head of the stairs, about to go into the bathroom. Her father answered it.

'David? Oh hello, Dave. No, no, she's in the bath I'm afraid. Then we're going out. We're going on a drive, into the country. A mate's lent me his car. Can I get her to ring you? Yes. Fine. Fine. Will do. Cheerioh.'

He put the receiver down and winked up the stairs.

'You terrible old liar,' Sandra laughed.

Lying in the bath, though, she didn't feel so good, or cheerful. She started to soap herself, but soon gave up, and stared morosely at the ceiling. Every so often she felt a small rush of panic, but mainly she felt worry, deep down sickening worry. It was obvious that David would do something, he had to. But what? And how could he do anything about the Mansoor case that would not come back to her? In the end it was inevitable. The people in the force were going to find out she was connected with a journalist, and had opened up her trap. Then what would happen?

The crazy thing was, that no one had ever told her *not* to talk. And if she was looking for a get-out, she could say, with absolute truth, that she did not know that anything was secret. She had assumed that Mohammed Mansoor had been arrested in the normal way, and would in due course be brought to book. What was unusual about that?

The trouble was, that although it was the absolute truth, there were other truths linked up with it. They were subtle ones, and delicate ones, but Sandra was not going to deny them. Not here, at any rate, in the comfort of her own mind. The police, for starters, were a closed society, with their own morality and rules. She'd been playing outside those rules, quite consciously, by keeping David secret. Because they did not know about him, it had probably never occurred to them that she did not know the ropes. She'd smelled a rat over Mansoor. She *had* smelled a rat. They had probably assumed that she had known the exact nature of the beast. And accepted it.

Sandra squirmed in the bath, and slooshed her hands around to keep the bits that were sticking out of the water warm. Fear of the consequences of David's knowledge was not all that was worrying her. There was what was happening in the case itself.

Suddenly, lying in the water became intolerable. She grabbed the sides of the bath and stood up. She had to be doing something. She needed something to occupy her mind. This was driving her crazy, she'd go and have a chat with Maggie. But as she rubbed herself vigorously with a towel, the thoughts kept crowding in. She'd been furious at Dave's suggestion that the police weren't trying, and yet she half suspected that there were elements of truth there somewhere, that the caravan might somehow *be* just a cover, as even the mythology of the Jackies said. She had told herself till she was sick of it that nothing bad was really happening in the cells, that policemen weren't really in the National Front, but she wasn't satisfied. She suddenly wondered if she'd blown the gaffe deliberately.

Sandra emerged from the bathroom in a rush of steam and a towel. As she swept across the landing the telephone caught her eye, downstairs. Perhaps she'd phone him. Perhaps she'd talk to David after all. Perhaps he was right. She hesitated, then let confusion win.

No, she'd go to Mag and Roger's for the day. Sod it. She needed company. And distraction.

After his second call to Sandra's house, David, too, became morose. But his mood did not last, for basically he was too excited. He did not believe that this would break them up, but after he'd had a cup of coffee, sitting by the telephone, he'd decided he didn't care anyway. It was impossible, sometimes, with Sandra in the police, it was ridiculous. And if she was going to carry on like this, and get herself involved in some of their nastier games, that would be that. Finito. Over.

Nevertheless, he toyed with the telephone for a good long time before he decided to make a move. He lived alone, in a small flat near the seafront, and he wished like mad that there was somebody to talk to, to chew the implications over with. He could go and see his Mum and Dad for Sunday lunch but that would do no good. His old man was high Tory, and if he knew what his son was thinking of there'd be hell to pay. In his eyes, the police could do no wrong, however hard they tried. And if they did, no one should admit it. It undermined morality.

The trouble was, that since he'd joined the paper, most of David's friends were journalists. And the last people he wanted to let this out to were them. He sensed a good old-fashioned scoop. An exclusive, crusading, story by David Tanner. He daydreamed of that for minutes on end. That would show old Renton, the Gauloise-smoking pseud.

At one stage David picked up the phone and dialled the police headquarters number. But before it rang out he put the receiver down. They weren't stupid, the police. If he asked them were they holding someone he'd get a variety of dusty answers. They knew all kinds of ways of telling less than truth. He didn't blame them for it, it was a useful ploy that journalists were good at too. He needed facts to hit them with. He needed something concrete.

Kenny Baby Shaw would be the other way. The idea hit him like a flash of light. My God, thought David, that would put the cat among the pigeons! That would get the coppers spitting blood! They hated him. Everybody did. He was the man who got things done.

Kenneth Shaw – called Kenny Baby always, no one quite knew why – was the city's race relations man. He was married to a black woman, and he ran the local racial equality campaign. He was the scourge of casual racists, and had attacked – publicly and very effectively – many city councillors and other dignitaries whom he'd caught out in varying degrees of racial nastiness. He wore a beard and denim, and he was extremely well-educated and articulate. He was one of the most hated people in town. David had never heard anyone respectable say a good word about him. With genuine excitement, he picked up the telephone directory.

Three shots in the dark – and one mouthful of abuse from another K. Shaw who was always being bothered – convinced David of the problem. Kenny Baby was ex-directory. He cursed, then rang a couple of his journalistic colleagues, framing the question very cagily. But they did not have the number. He sat and cursed again, furious. It would have to wait.

David couldn't, though. If he could not set on the dogs of war, he'd do some solid groundwork in the meantime. He got on his shoes and jacket, and headed for his garage. Soon he was making for Hindley Lane End, humming tunelessly in time to the windscreen wipers.

As he drove he thought of Sandra, then dismissed her from his mind. If she got into trouble over it, that was that. He had his job to do, it couldn't be helped. In any case, she wouldn't. She was far too smart. Why should they blame it on her just because the Press were sniffing about? He didn't believe she'd chuck him up, either, not over this. Although he recognised, with a vaguely sinking feeling, that their relationship was already under tremendous strain. He remembered last Sunday, in the woods, and shivered. He hoped she wouldn't, anyway . . .

He wasn't quite sure what he was expecting, but he was disappointed, whatever it was. Tuebrook Road was deserted in the rain, not even any children hanging around. And No. 27 was empty.

He stood outside for minutes, his jacket getting rather soggy rather rapidly, and water dripping from his hair. He raised the knocker and banged again. But the house even sounded empty. Hollow. At last he tried the next door. A little Asian woman in a sari opened it.

'Excuse me,' he said. 'I'm from the *Evening Echo*. Is Mrs Mansoor in? Can you tell me where she has gone?'

She smiled nervously, but did not speak. After two minutes he repeated what he had said, more slowly. The woman smiled some more, nodding. But still she did not speak. He felt absurd.

In the end, David mumbled politely, and backed off, dripping water. He felt a complete fool, idiotic. He went and sat in the Metro, wondering what to do. He half got out, at one point, to try another door. Then he sat back, embarrassed. The little lady in the sari was staring at him from her downstairs window, the curtain pulled aside.

'Gawd,' said David. 'The famous newshound strikes. This is ridiculous.'

He glanced at his watch. Half past twelve. His coat was sopping.

'I'm going for a pint,' he muttered. 'Change my clothes and go and have a pint. This is ridiculous.'

EIGHT

David knew he was onto something big, and he worked at it like a demon. But it was two days before he got his story. He knew he'd finally cracked it when the phone on his desk rang late on Tuesday morning. It was Kenny Baby Shaw, and it was a confirmation call. He outlined what his organisation had in mind, and he ended by thanking David. David replaced the receiver and grinned happily. He thrust his legs out in the kneehole of his desk and stretched backwards, luxuriously. Anne Higgins, who was walking past with a coffee in her hand, stopped and smiled.

'What are you looking so happy about?' she said. 'You look like the cat that got the cream.'

'I am,' said David. 'No. Not the cat that got the cream. I, Miss Higgins, *am* the cream. Just you wait and see.'

He got up and sauntered to the newsdesk. Sam Renton was scribbling in the diary, a Disque Bleu hanging from his lip in the manner of a Parisian roadworker. He did not look up, and David observed his thick-haired head with satisfaction.

'Excuse me, Sam,' he said. 'Sorry to bother you, but I think I ought to pop down to Union Street. I think there might be something coming off. Any minute now.'

Renton looked up and took the cigarette from his mouth. He coughed.

'What's that, flower? Like what, for instance?'

'Mohammed Mansoor,' said David. And stopped.

Renton's eyes narrowed, but he was too smart, unfortunately, to take David's bait. It was a sore subject between them now – and specifically a closed one. It was *verboten* to mention it.

'I take it, David,' he said coolly, 'that there's been a development. I suppose it's in the nature of things that I'll end up with egg on my face.'

David grinned. It was as near to a climbdown as he was ever likely to hear. It was enough.

'I've just had Kenny Baby on the line,' he said. 'Shaw, the race relations king. They've got the full story and they've got their legal man on the move. According to him, Mansoor's been inside headquarters more than a week. Since the murder. No charges, no witnesses, no access to a solicitor, nix. Totally, utterly, and completely illegal. It's a cracker.'

Renton whistled.

'If it's true,' he said, 'it's a ball-tearer. Dynamite. Kenny Baby, eh? How the hell did *he* get in on it, I wonder.'

Keep wondering, thought David happily. I'm not telling you.

'Habeus corpus,' he said quickly, in case Renton made the connection. David was not sure, but he suspected that the newseditor would not take kindly to what he'd done. News was there to be gathered, not manipulated. 'If they get no joy this morning, they'll be seeking a writ immediately.'

'Damn me,' said Renton. He crushed his cigarette end out and lit another one, striking the match on the desk top as usual. He took a deep drag and blew the smoke out into the long and noisy newsroom. His phone rang and he called out to a passing reporter to take it. 'Damn me,' he repeated. 'And what did the buggers say yesterday?'

'The police?' said David. 'They were holding no one. I've been trying to confirm this since Sunday, in fact. Since I got the tip-off. They swore black was white they were holding no one.'

'Lying sods,' said Renton. 'Though it was probably strictly true, of course. They'll swear black was white *now* that he was always free to go. I wonder if they'll charge him. It looks as if they'll have to. That or let him out. Amazing.'

'It wouldn't have happened to a white man, that's for sure,' said David, craftily. 'It's appalling.'

Renton looked at him levelly, from under bushy brows.

'Yeah,' he said. Again he left the bait. 'You'd better get down there, sunshine, and watch the action.'

Five minutes later, David was in the orange Metro. He listened to the news on Seawave with deep satisfaction. Nothing. That had been the deal with Kenny Baby. He'd got his story and it would be exclusive. Seawave and the rest could follow up that night. He prayed they wouldn't charge the kid – which would make all forms of comment a heck of a lot more dicey – but he didn't think they would. It was a pound to a penny he was innocent. A pound to a penny.

David had finally got in touch with Shaw on Monday lunchtime. He'd spent the morning trying to wring an admission from the police, and he'd had a row with Renton for asking several times if he could drive down to Hindley Lane End. Renton – whom he had not told about the Mohammed tip, in case he gave the investigation to a more senior man – was adamant that the story was dead. He was not going to have his reporters wasting their time on wild goose chases, he said, and at last issued his edict: the Mansoor case was a banned subject. David was to drop it, or there'd be trouble.

That had given David pause for thought. He wasn't sure just what the retribution might be if he broke the rule, but he had to take it seriously. On the other hand, though, it had made him even more determined. After ten minutes, he'd left the newsroom and walked to the pay phone in the front office. He'd dialled the number of the racial equality campaign offices. And when Shaw was on the line, had spoken conspiratorially, cupping his hand around the mouthpiece anxiously.

'Hello,' he'd said. 'My name's . . . No, never mind that. I want to talk to you.'

Kenny Baby Shaw sounded slightly bored.

'Then talk,' he'd said. 'There's no one stopping you.'

David was taken aback, then realised the campaign

probably got many calls from cranks. He cleared his throat.

'Look,' he said. 'It's about the Mansoor murder. There's something I think you ought to know. But I can't talk like this. Can we meet?'

'Listen, what is this?' said Shaw, impatiently. 'Why can't you speak?'

'Because it's more than my job's worth,' said David. 'I'm a reporter. On the *Echo*. And I'm in the office. Look. The police are holding the Mansoor boy. Mohammed. I can't prove it but I know it's true. All right?'

There had been a long pause. Then Kenny Baby Shaw had made a date. An hour later they'd met in the Commercial Hotel, in town.

Despite his reputation, Kenneth Shaw was impressive. He was accompanied by a man David found even more so – a black. This was Riccard, a sombre West Indian with a full beard who stared broodingly and spoke very little. He was an activist of many years standing, and a Marxist. When he was mentioned by the *Echo* – and they tried to avoid it – it was in scathing terms. He was a militant, an extremist, according to their leader writer, and it was his sort who did most harm to race relations in the town. If people like he and Kenny Baby Shaw would only keep their mouths shut, what few problems there were would surely go away. By keeping them in the open, in the public eye, the pair of them exacerbated matters. They made a minor irritation a running sore.

David, in his keenness to show them whose side he was on, went over the top, rather. He told them what he knew quickly and concisely, but he couldn't resist referring to the Mansoor affair as a racial murder, and said it was a clear case of the police deliberately harrassing an innocent black.

Kenny Baby Shaw and Riccard exchanged glances. David was rather hurt by their apparent coolness.

'Don't you think you might be jumping the gun a little?' asked Kenny Baby Shaw.

'Just because the police hold him illegally, does not mean

55

he's innocent.' Riccard had a heavy voice, with a faint West Indian accent. What he said made David blink.

'Oh. Well. I . . .' He paused, confused. This was hardly the reaction of a Marxist firebrand.

Kenny Baby said: 'I think we'd better take it step by step. There's no percentage in getting furious. I'll set the procedures in motion immediately. We'll get the legal eagles on it. I'll call you, in strict confidence, of course, when there's something concrete. And thanks for the tip-off.'

He and Riccard stood up. David blushed.

'My pleasure,' he said. 'I think it's scandalous, actually. Well, on the surface I . . . Well.'

They were moving away, smiling politely, distantly.

'Have another drink,' he said. 'No need to rush away. I'm on my lunchbreak.'

They exchanged a glance once more.

'Thanks all the same,' said Riccard. 'We're busy. See you, huh?'

'Yeah,' said David. He was still red. He hid his face in his pint pot as they left.

It was another mistake, coming to the station. He guessed Renton had known he'd get nowhere, but had let him try in the hope he'd be humiliated. A neat way of getting his own back. The sergeant in the information room, now he had David's face to look at instead of just hearing him on the phone, was frostier than the Arctic. He still skated round the fact of Mansoor's questioning, he refused to acknowledge that the race equality campaign had been in touch, he denied categorically that they were in the building even now. After ten minutes David, furious and biting his lip in embarrassment, made his escape. As he drove back to the office and the safety of the phone, he got as close as a toucher to admitting it: he had a lot to learn.

Mohammed Mansoor was lying in his cell, exhausted, dirty, and in agony. It was mental agony, mostly, and it had to do with his mother, and his family. His father had receded to

56

the farthest corners of his mind, despite the fact that he was the only person the policemen ever talked about. But his mother was alone, lost, and must be suffering. How many days was it? He did not even know. The neighbours were the only hope, in Mohammed Mansoor's mind. If they were not helping her, his mother's fate was unthinkable.

He raised his head listlessly when the cell door opened, and his body tensed. But for once, amazingly, he was not being taken for interrogation, or abuse. It was a doctor there, he thought. A man in a white coat. Five minutes later, to his astonishment, he was in a shower. And after it, he got clean clothes. What could have happened?

Kenny Baby Shaw and Riccard *had* been in headquarters, and the effect had been extraordinary. Sandra, her stint in the caravan mercifully, if mysteriously, over – no one ever told you why duties changed, it happened merely – was back in the filing room with Jackie One. Jackie Two was in the caravan, and Sandra wished her well of it. News travelled in the station like wildfire, always, and it wasn't long before Jackie One returned from the Ladies full of it.

'Sandra,' she said, excitedly. 'That Kenny Shaw's been in! With that Commie Rastus, or Rasputin or whatever he calls himself! Hell, gal! There'll be ructions!'

Sandra sat down wearily, glad of an excuse to stop the filing.

'Why?' she asked. 'What've they done? What're they in for?' She had to play it very cool. Her stomach had left her with a lurch. This would be David's doing, it had to be.

'They're not *inside*, you twit, they've been *in*,' said Jackie One. 'And whatever it is, it'll mean trouble. They're poison, those two are. They're murder. It's over Mansoor, it's got to be.'

Sandra said carefully: 'Can they do anything? I mean, we haven't done anything wrong, or anything, have we? I mean, we've only arrested someone for murder, haven't we?'

'Oh yeah, no trouble, they can't get us, we're fireproof,'

said Jackie One. She didn't sound exactly sure, though. She extracted a cigarette from her packet on the table, and puffed thoughtfully.

'But then again, you never know for certain,' she said. 'I mean, with these blacks you can't be too careful, like I told you. It's a real problem when you've got a job to do, like us. It's not easy. It's not so easy at all . . .'

Whatever the ins and outs of it, things for Mohammed Mansoor changed rapidly. As the station buzzed with rumour and counter rumour throughout the long afternoon, his life became miraculously better. He wasn't exactly mollycoddled, or patted on the head and sent home or anything, but a cloud of fear and misery was slowly lifted from him. By four fifteen he felt a different person. Things were not perfect, by any means. But they were changing.

At four fifteen he was moved to a different cell, a larger one, which was cleaner – much cleaner – than the one he'd grovelled in for ages. As he was moved from one side of Union Street headquarters to the other, he came face to face with Sandra.

It was one of those weird coincidences. She had not been seeking the meeting, rubbernecking like some of her colleagues wanted to. She and Jackie One were merely returning from their tea break, where they'd had coffee and scones and chatted with their neighbours about Shaw, and Rastus, and Mohammed Mansoor.

The two of them turned the corner of a corridor, and there he was, unhandcuffed, between two large constables. Sandra almost passed out. She turned quite pale, and gasped. Mohammed Mansoor jumped, also, and he made a startled noise in his throat. Then he was gone, round the corner with his escort.

'What's up, love?' said Jackie. 'You look as if you've seen a ghost. That's our little murderer, Mohammed. Pretty, isn't he?'

'But I know him,' said Sandra. She was shattered, amazed. 'I went to school with him.

'It's Noor Allahi.'

NINE

To give credit where it was due, David had to admit that Sam Renton went to town when he was sure he had a story. Although it was fairly late on before they got confirmation that the police *were* holding Mansoor, the wheels had been already set in motion. The editor and the chief sub had designed a stand-by front page in case everything came through in time, and a large section of the centre news spread was available if David managed to get a good background piece.

Although the information room at Union Street appeared determined to keep up their rearguard action for as long as possible, after the visit by Shaw and his team a statement was inevitable. They knew all about the *Echo*'s edition times, and stalled bravely. But while David was despatched to try and interview the murdered man's widow, Renton tackled headquarters. He worked his way slowly up from the information room to chief superintendent level, and he threatened him with going to the Chief Constable. He furthermore said that unless there was either a charge or an explanation he would go ahead in any case. For the police, there was only one action that could lessen the impact: charging Mohammed Mansoor. He was not charged.

David parked the Metro in Tuebrook Road with a mixture of fear and excitement in his stomach. He was actually praying as he walked to the front door of No. 27 and knocked. The fingers on both his hands were tightly crossed.

After only a few seconds he heard footsteps inside. There was the sound of a bolt being drawn – which he noted as significant ('Mrs Mansoor lives in fear') – then the door opened on a chain. A brown and timid face peered out.

'Hello,' he said, nervously. 'My name is David Tanner. I am from the *Evening Echo*. I wanted to have a few words with you, please.'

Remembering his experiences with the lady next door, David could only hope. If this one was a deaf-mute, or couldn't speak English or whatever, he was finished. She did, in fact, look at him for what felt like minutes before she answered.

'No,' she said. 'Thank you, sir. Not talk.'

Her English was slow, and very heavily accented. She was tiny, and peered up at him through the crack.

'I am from the paper,' said David, slowly and carefully. 'I am a reporter. I have come to help.'

There was still no response. David heard a noise behind Mrs Mansoor and a small brown face appeared in the crack as well. A bright-eyed, curious, face.

'What do you want?' it said. 'Are you a copper? Where's my brother?'

David laughed.

'No, I'm not a copper,' he said. 'I'm from the *Echo*, the local paper. I've got news of your brother, though. Mohammed. I've come to talk to your Mummy.'

The woman's face changed.

'Mohammed?' she said. 'You know Mohammed? Where he is? Is he . . .? Is he . . .?'

The little boy said eagerly: 'Is Noor all right? Is he in prison? Will he come home soon?'

It took a few more minutes, but with some help from the boy, David managed to get through to Mrs Mansoor. He told them where Mohammed was, he told them steps were being taken, and he said they had to talk to him. The publicity would help, he said. The affair must be brought into the open. The authorities would be forced to act. He could hardly credit what they seemed to be saying, that they did not know where Mohammed was, it was incredible. But the woman was confused, and frightened, and trembling: it probably was not so. In the end the chain was taken off and she backed nervously away. The little boy, who was in jeans and a tee-shirt, beckoned him inside.

He was taken into the front room, which was dark and gloomy, with the heavy curtains tightly drawn. The floor was bare, oddly, and although there were two armchairs, there was no sofa. It hit David with a shock, after a few seconds, that this was the room where Mansoor had been killed. Oh my God, he thought, how strange that they still use it. The carpet and the sofa must have been taken out.

The little boy's name was Rafiq – Raf for short, he said brightly – and he was eight. He didn't go to school much at the moment, he went on, because of Mummy. She had his little sister to look after, and she was not well. She was upset. She was always crying since Noor was taken by the police. His sister was in bed, asleep. She was not yet four.

As if on cue, Mrs Mansoor began to cry. She did so quietly, with her head bent low and her face hidden in one hand. Rafiq looked at her calmly but did not move to comfort her.

'You see?' he said to David.

David did, but tried not to look, out of politeness. He was tremendously excited, with a faint touch of shame because of it. It was odd, being a reporter. He knew he'd found something dreadful, an awful piece of human misery, and his main reaction was elation. What a story!

It was. Rafiq told it, with the occasional interjection from his mother, usually in a language that David took to be Urdu. He told it completely unvarnished, and without any visible emotion. David was fascinated. To the boy, obviously, the strange events were just part of what happened. If he'd been frightened and upset by any of it at the time, he'd either forgotten it or got used to it. Even the fact that his father was dead did not appear to worry him all that much. As with his brother, the disappearance probably just seemed unreal. One day, Rafiq probably assumed, they would both appear again. Just like that, as large as life.

With David questioning carefully, it emerged that the boy, the girl and the mother had returned on the afternoon of the murder to find the place swarming with policemen. There had been an ambulance outside and they had not been allowed into the room, or to see his brother. His mother had become hysterical, there had been screaming and shouting, and at last his brother had been taken away. For hours, late into the night, the police had stayed, but they could not understand his mother and they would not talk to him. It had been terrible. In the end they had been left alone, in the house where his Daddy had been killed. The next day and the next the police had come back and there had been much trouble and misery. They had taken things away, furniture and clothes and belongings, and they had broken and spoiled many things, in their searching. Always they had refused to explain.

Since that time, many days ago, they had heard nothing. No one had come, no police had called. They did not know where Noor was, or what had happened to him.

'But didn't you see a lawyer?' asked David. 'Didn't you try and . . .?' He realised the words were foolish, pointless. Rafiq smiled at him, questioningly. He was a kid. A little boy.

Mrs Mansoor, who had followed it all as best she could, and who was no longer crying, said simply: 'They think Noor kill his *chacha*. It is not. Noor kill nobody.'

'No,' said David. 'I'm sure you are right.' He smiled, comfortingly. 'Why do you call him Noor?' he asked Rafiq. 'You keep calling him Noor. Isn't his name Mohammed?'

Rafiq nodded.

'If you like,' he said. 'Most English call him Mohammed Mansoor because Daddy's name is Mansoor. He has another name, we call him. Noor Allahi.'

David didn't understand, and he tried to clarify it. Yes, agreed Rafiq, he was his brother. Yes, Mrs Mansoor was his mother and Mr Mansoor, Yusuf, his father. They were all the one family. So why did he have a different name? Well, he did. What was wrong with that? He was called Noor Allahi, he always had been. David got quite frustrated, but Raf was only eight and he couldn't see a problem. David decided to drop it. For his story, Mohammed Mansoor would be just that, as he always had been. What a funny business.

He looked at his watch and started. Hell. He'd have to get his skates on. He thought of the big space in the centre pages, waiting for his copy. He snapped his notebook shut and thanked them very much. He stuck his hand out to Mrs Mansoor, but she only looked at it, shyly. He felt a rush of affection.

'Don't worry, love,' he said. 'We'll get him out, you see if we don't. This is fantastic, amazing, terrible. We'll save him for you. We'll show them.'

She smiled, not understanding. He headed for the door.

'See you, kid,' he said to Rafiq. 'Get tonight's paper and read it to your Mum. It'll be fantastic.'

'Yeah,' said Raf. 'But I can't read properly yet. See you, Mister.'

He closed the door.

The story made it in the late city edition, and Sandra was in the station when the reaction broke. It had been an odd time for her in any case, since coming face to face with Noor Allahi. But the storm of outrage shook her even more.

After Noor had disappeared around the corner, Jackie One had looked at her most strangely.

'What do you mean, Noor Allahi?' she asked. 'That's miladdo. That's Mohammed Mansoor, the murderer. Who's Noor Allahi when he's out?'

Sandra felt too hollow to talk. She mumbled, almost incoherently.

'I went to school with him. It never occurred to me. Oh my God, how terrible.'

Jackie waited as patiently as she could. She took Sandra's arm and steered her back to their filing room. She sat her down and tried to make her take a fag, which Sandra refused. When she was a little calmer, Jackie tried again. This time Sandra got it out.

'I'd forgotten,' she said. 'Well, it never occurred to me in fact. There was always a bit of confusion at school, as well. I'd forgotten that was his other name. Mansoor. Mohammed Mansoor. But his name's Allahi. We always called him Noor Allahi. Oh my God.'

'D'you mean that the old guy wasn't his father, then?' said Jackie One. 'D'you mean they're not related?'

'Oh no,' said Sandra. 'It's just a custom thing, or something. Religion or something, I dunno. No, that's his dad all right. Was. They just had different names.'

'It's a riot, isn't it?' said Jackie gloomily. 'What a bleeding performance. They all flood over here to live and turn us upside down. Two names? It's impossible.'

Sandra wasn't listening. She felt dreadful. Poor little Noor. She'd never known him, properly, he was a bit of a weed. And anyway, she'd never had much to do with the blacks, she was indifferent. But it brought it home to her, somehow. My God, what he must have gone through. Even if he had killed his father. And she couldn't believe it, really, now. Not little weedy Noor.

When the *Evening Echo* reached the station, little weedy Noor started an explosion. A wave of fury swept through Union Street that was almost palpable. More copies were sent out for, and soon small knots of policemen and women had gathered in several places to discuss it. Some of the groups were vociferous, even noisy, and senior officers had to shut them up. They did it sympathetically, though. They could understand the rage. They shared it.

The front page had a banner headline that said: 'Scandal of the "lost" days.' Underneath it was a smaller headline that went on: 'Mohammed held in secret after brutal murder – no charges.' In big, bold type the story began: 'Mohammed Mansoor, 17-year-old son of murder victim Yusuf Mansoor, has been held in secret custody by the City police for more than a week. No charges have been brought against him.' It went on to detail how the information had come to light, how Mohammed's mother, who spoke little English and had no relatives in Britain to turn to, had been left alone with two children, and how Mr Kenneth Shaw, of the racial equality campaign, had taken up the case. A panel at the foot of the page referred to the centre page interview with the 'tragic woman' whose husband had been savagely murdered, whose son had been taken away, and who had been told nothing, absolutely nothing, by the police.

It was the sight of Kenny Shaw's name that infuriated them most. It was generally agreed that it was a plot between the Press and the 'race relations industry'. They were all deeply hurt by it. Angry, depressed, and hurt. Sandra found the whole thing strange, bizarre. She knew the facts as reported were true, but she dared not say so. She was only glad, and grateful, that in the confusion, no one ever bothered to wonder how the *Echo* and Shaw had come to know about it. If she kept her mouth shut she would yet escape.

That evening, she went out with Brian in his car. He kept a sports jacket and a pair of casual shoes in the boot and Sandra, as before, took off her tights and tie. They sat outside the pub they'd found the last time, although the evening was not sunny, merely warm and overcast. Brian's rule about staying off police work was forgotten. The copy of the late city *Echo* lay between them on the bench.

At first, Brian was inclined to carry on the tirade that Sandra had heard before. It was a media plot, he said. The TV and the nationals would latch onto it tomorrow, all hell would break loose. He, like everybody else, was outraged most by the suggestions of police misconduct.

'Jesus Christ,' he said. 'Just what do they *want* of us, what do they *want*? Some bloody nignog kills his Dad and we're meant to treat him like the Pope? All right, he'd had it bad. He's been roughed up a bit, lost a bit of sleep. What else do they expect? Do they think criminals are like you and me or something? Do they think you say "You killed your Dad", and he says "Yes, of course I did, sorry"? They're crazy. Crazy.'

Sandra was disturbed by some of it – the roughing up, for

instance, the 'nignog' bit – but she said nothing. She felt tired and depressed and she guessed that Brian did too. His face was strained, and sad, and he appeared bemused at whose side everyone was on. It was a theme that had recurred and recurred at headquarters.

'Everyone's against us,' he said. 'Everyone. That bastard Kenny Baby Shaw just wants to put us down, he'd do anything to stick the knife in, and those purblind fools on the *Echo* eat out of his hand. Can't they see what he's doing? He's out to destroy, he's a leftie, an anarchist, he wants destruction. At any price. The blacks are just his weapon, his device. And it works. This society's rotting, Sandra, it's falling to bits. We're in the front line, the thin blue line. We're trying to save the place from anarchy, the whole flaming boiling. And everyone's against us.'

He drank deeply from his pint. He was less angry now, his voice was leveller.

'It's not just the Kenny Babies, though,' he said. 'It's not just the Rastuses of this world. It's everything. Some rotten little thug kicks in an old lady for eighteen pence and what does he get? Probation. Some football hooligans break up a train and terrorise two hundred innocent people with rocks and bottles and what do they get? Banned from the terraces for three home matches. It's appalling. It's sickening. And no one seems to care. What about the Yorkshire Ripper, there's a case in point. Five years, billions of hours, and millions of quid. And when we finally nail the bastard the Press have a field day, a jamboree, because they reckon we should have found him sooner. Half the male population could have done it, he chose his own times, his own places, his own rules – and when we catch him we're stupid bastards. It's diabolical, Sandra love. It's diabolical.'

Later, sitting in the front seats of the car on the hill, looking out over the lights of the city glittering like jewels on a black velvet tray, Sandra listened to much more. It was as though Brian had not talked for years. His voice was quiet and soft, and his residual rage over the *Echo* had long before turned to an expression of pessimism and pain. He thought the whole thing hopeless, society was lost and hopeless. The police were decent men, ordinary human beings trying to do a job that was getting worse and worse and worse. And if they put so much as one foot wrong, over anything, they were jumped on. By the Press, by the politicians, by everyone. If they hit criminals hard, or rioters, or thugs, or looters, they were over-reacting. If they tried the soft approach they were failing in their duty. No one had a good word for them, ever. They had to save society, and if they made just one mistake, even their masters kicked them. He wanted to serve with pride, he said. He knew he was different, that being in the force made you different, better, aloof; in a class alone, and above the ruck. But you were looked upon as scum, for trying to do your duty. It was hopeless.

Sandra felt sad and tender, listening to the words, watching his profile in the faint light from the sky. She felt desperately sorry for him, somehow. She could not put it into words. His hands on the steering wheel were strong and hard, but they moved her deeply.

It was very late when he stopped talking at last. They wound the reclining seats down together, not speaking, and made love.

TEN

It was the next afternoon before Noor Allahi was released, with no apologies made and no reasons given. The general buzz was that the forensic boys had ruled him out, and the circumstantial case against him just wasn't strong enough to stand up a charge. Whether or not the national Press and the television would have followed up the scandal angle, however, became a dead letter. For shortly after the release, one of those random events happened that for Sandra made police work so interesting. She was involved, and it was an appalling tragedy. Which ended in the death of a colleague.

The afternoon was brilliantly sunny, and when Sandra managed to throw off the feeling of gloomy foreboding she had left over from the previous evening, she enjoyed it a lot. The memory – and the worry – faded gradually as she toured the town with Terry and his oppo, Tony Gardiner. Terry was on form, and steered the conversation away from difficult topics – like race, and Mohammed Mansoor – as far as possible. He had sensed that morning that Sandra was keyed up, and he had engineered for her to spend her shift with him. Sandra had been grateful. She'd been terrified she would have been linked with Brian for the day, and she was not sure she could handle it.

Late the night before, back home in her bed, she had tried to think through exactly what had happened, and why. Her relationship with David was over, surely? They fought like cat and dog, they hardly saw each other. Making love with Brian was not disloyal, anyway. Nobody owned her. It had been a natural thing, a reaching out between them. But she couldn't convince herself, try as she might. She ended up yearning for David. She missed him desperately. It was ages before she slept.

By mid-afternoon, they were down on the seafront. The Panda was parked on the promenade, almost like a tripper's car. All around them, in fact, were trippers, thousands of them, trippers and holidaymakers and kids. All the windows of the car were open and they were enjoying the sun, smiling in a friendly fashion to passing mums and children. Terry was mopping his brow with a big coloured handkerchief, and Sandra was complaining about what a drag it was to have to wear black tights on such a blazing day, when the news came through on Tony's radio, clipped to his jacket in the back. He interrupted Sandra angrily.

'Good God above,' he said. 'Would you credit it? The murdering little swine's got away with it. They've sprung Mansoor.'

Sandra felt her body tensing. Tony Gardiner wasn't exactly known as a liberal, for all he was Terry's mate. She said nothing, staring way across the green water. It looked so peaceful.

Terry said moderately: 'If they've let him go, Tony, it probably means he didn't do it, cock. You know that.'

'Do I hell,' said Tony, heatedly. 'It means we couldn't nail the sod, that's all. Slimy little Paki. It makes me sick. If that little git didn't kill his father I'll eat my hat.'

Terry started the engine and began to back cautiously out into the stream of traffic.

'Whichever way you look at it,' he grunted, 'we couldn't hang on to the lad. Not without a charge. Not now the Press was on to it.'

'Yeah,' said Tony. 'They're the ones I blame. They're the ones who blew it. He'd have cracked in the end, no danger. If there's a killer on the loose, it's down to them in the last analysis. It's bloody down to them.'

There was silence for a while as they drove. Sandra hoped the subject would be dropped, and she cast around for something else to talk about. But nothing came.

As they drove down the long wide cobbled route to the

commercial docks – well away from the holidaymakers' haunts – Tony's radio crackled again. It told them of a coastguard call. A small motorboat in difficulty in the harbour, being swept towards the entrance on the ebb. It didn't appear to have anything to do with them, but Terry took a left turn that would lead them to a vantage point. They might as well take a look, when all was said. There was nothing else particular to do.

'Anyway,' he said to Tony, when he'd found the right road. 'I think you're barking up the wrong tree on our little dusky friend. He was downstairs for long enough, with Ted Winter, too. It's a wonder the poor little devil was capable of walking out of the station. It looked to me, Tony lad, as if the boy was innocent.'

Gardiner laughed good-naturedly. He and Terry had been friends for years.

'Yah, you soft bastard,' he said. 'You'd have let old Crippen off, you would. Just because he wore glasses! Innocent my left leg!'

'Ah well,' said Terry, turning onto the dockside. 'No point in arguing with a fascist hyena.'

'I'm not a fascist,' said Tony. 'I'm a Social Democrat extremist!'

The two of them were still chuckling when Terry drew the Panda to a halt on the point of the dockside overlooking the harbour, and Sandra was smiling too. They all three got out and started to scan the bright waters. Terry spotted the boat almost at once. He pointed.

'Look,' he said. 'Up there by that big tanker effort. Small green job. Can you see it?'

Sandra picked it out in the end, and so did Tony Gardiner. She couldn't see that it was in much danger. It just looked like a boat to her. But Tony, beside her, got quite agitated.

'Hell, Terry,' he said. 'She's in trouble that one. Someone's got to move, fast.'

Terry, like Sandra, was ignorant of boats.

'What's up?' he asked. 'What's the problem, then?'

'The tide, you twerp,' said Gardiner. 'It's going like an express train. If they're not careful they're going to end up jammed between the hulks. Look. See. Those two huge old things moored on the battleship buoys. If that boat gets pushed onto those chains, she's finished. She'll roll over like a peapod down a stormdrain. They'll go under those two hulks.'

Sandra saw the danger. Although the motorboat was a few hundred yards up-tide of the hulks, it was moving fast towards them. It did look, even to her, as if it was going to end up jammed between the two high bows.

Gardiner leapt into the car and spoke urgently on the radio clipped to his jacket. He came out thirty seconds later looking agitated.

'The lifeboat's on its way but it'll never make it, never,' he said. 'It's way outside the harbour, two, three miles. It's far too late. Come on!'

Sandra and Terry, feeling rather like spare parts, followed as he hurried round the dock wall. They left the Panda unlocked and unattended. About a hundred yards away, round the corner, was a small dock basin, where the inshore fishing boats and other small motor vessels moored. There were several men at work on their boats, or sitting in the sun. Tony jumped lightly off the dockside onto the foredeck of one of them.

As Terry and Sandra looked at each other, half perplexed, half amused, Tony explained the situation. The man moved fast, and less than a minute later, the engine thudded into life. He and Tony scrabbled with her mooring lines, and Tony shouted up at them impatiently: 'Come on then, for God's sake! Get on board!'

It was extraordinary. Hardly before she knew it, she was on the motor boat, heading for the entrance to the basin. The engine rumbled noisily, the boat swayed, and the wind blew in her face and hair, fresh smelling, salty, beautiful. Tony was on his personal radio, which he'd grabbed from his jacket, telling HQ what was happening. She looked around her, quite elated. It was fantastic!

They rounded the corner into the open harbour and began punching against the tide towards the hulks. The water was busy, with two or three cargo boats on the move, the pale blue ferry heading in a wide arc from one side to the other, and several gaily-painted pleasure launches, crowded with holidaymakers, chugging up the lines of ships moored along the docksides. Nobody else was apparently aware that the motor boat was in trouble.

Sandra looked at it as they slowly moved nearer, but it was hard to share the urgency of Tony and the boatman. The sun was so warm, the smell of the sea and the odd burst of spray over the bows were so pleasant. She was enjoying it, no question. As the green boat drifted out of view behind the hulks it seemed totally unreal. They couldn't be in *actual* danger, it was impossible.

As they moved up the great black sides of the hulks, which were used as overnight moorings for the ferry boats, she could see the speed the tide was moving at. There were flecks of white all along the sides, and a trailing rope was pointing down-harbour and splashing and twirling in the current. Tony took the wheel, and the boatman got Terry to help him with a coil of heavy rope. She guessed they would need it for a tow.

It must have taken nearly fifteen minutes to reach the bows of the hulks from the basin. As they passed the huge old battleship buoys the whole picture suddenly changed. Even Sandra could see how dangerous it was. She went white.

The tide rip into the triangular gap between the pair of bows was awful. The hulks were tethered to the massive buoys with enormous, rusty chains. The ones leading upwards were taut, taking all the strain, but there were others, leading back, and sagging deep into the water. Onto one of these sunk chains, that rose and sawed at the swirling harbour surface as the hulks moved uneasily on the tide, the small green boat was being inexorably pushed.

The boatman had taken the wheel once more, and Tony, Terry and Sandra were standing near the foredeck, looking back into the chasm between the hulks. As they did so the

72

green boat, as if made of something very light, was lifted by the rising chain. It began to slowly roll, between the chain and the tide, until one rounded bilge, broadside on across the rip, was presented to them. As it turned turtle two men clambered frantically onto the high side, as if they were walking on a rolling barrel. Neither of them was young, they were middle-aged, unwieldy. Their faces were rigid with fear, and one of them was black.

'Jesus, Tony,' said Terry, with uneasy humour. 'You're going to have to help a coon. There's a turn-up for the book.'

But Tony was not listening. He was tearing off his clothes, with almost frantic haste. The boatman, without needing any instructions, was heading the tide and dropping slowly backwards towards the wreck, judging his engine speed with caution and precision. He was old, with a weather-battered, lined face. His lips were stiff with concentration.

Tony, in his underpants, picked up the heavy line and moved towards the stern.

'Tie it round you, Tony, tie it round,' shouted Terry.

'Can you hold her steady?' called the boatman, glancing round at Terry and indicating the wheel. As he turned, the boat began to slew across the tide, and he cursed, and hit the throttle. The engine noise rose, and he fought the boat back into position. His question went unanswered. No, of course Terry could not. Tony and the boatman were on their own.

As the little motor boat rolled right over, the two men jumped. They were both in only jeans, and barefooted, presumably having partly stripped in the last minutes before being dragged into the trap. They both managed to grab a chain, the black man a high, taut one, and his companion a sunken one. He held it at the point where it entered the water, and the tearing, rushing tide immediately submerged him. His head broke surface a second or two later, and his eyes were rolling, he was coughing water. He dragged and clawed his way a few links further up the chain, towards the buoy. Then he disappeared once more. The black man, his heavy, fattish body hanging by his hands, rose up and down in a ghastly, tearing movement, sometimes completely in the air, his feet not even in the water, sometimes dipping almost to his shoulders.

In the seconds that Sandra was watching, horrified, the small green motor boat was rolled right under. There was a crunching and splintering, a grinding, tearing noise. The tide crushed it down, between the bows and under them. It was swallowed whole, incredibly to her. She could not imagine such power, that sun-drenched water could do it to a boat. It was unimaginable.

Tony decided to save the white man first, because he was in such terrible danger. He wrapped the heavy rope round his wrist and lowered himself over the stern. Terry, anguished, said: 'Tony, tie it, man. For God's sake tie it round your *waist*.'

But Tony, as he bobbed away, flashed him a grim smile. 'Won't work,' he said. 'Tony knows best. Just stand by at that Samson-post. Keep the turns on, whatever you do.'

Terry and Sandra held the rope – wound twice round the Samson-post as Tony had shown them – and paid it out until he had reached the white man. He was almost finished, it was quite plain to both of them. Tony clung onto the chain, as high out of the water as he could, and unwound the rope from his wrist. The other man, looking already like a drowned fish, hung there, the water flowing and bursting over his face and head. It seemed ages before Tony had tied the rope to him, and placed part of it in his hands. He raised an arm to signal, and shot underwater himself. But by the time Terry and Sandra started hauling, he had reappeared.

Within half a minute, Terry and Sandra were in pain. With the help of the turns round the Samson-post, they managed to haul the rope in, six-inch by six-inch. But it was killing work. Sandra's nails broke up one by one, and she noticed at one point that her hand was bleeding. Terry, luckily, although fat, was very strong and fit. The sweat poured off him, bathed his stolid red face. Sandra's skirt tore, and her bra-strap burst. She thought her lungs would burst.

74

Somehow they got the first man to the stern, which mercifully was low. He still had just the strength to help as Terry hauled him inboard. He crashed into the bottom of the boat and lay there, vomiting water, choking. Terry rolled him roughly to one side and turned back to the stern.

The black man and Tony were now in roughly similar danger. Tony had worked himself further along the chain, so that his head rarely went under. But when Terry and Sandra returned to their task he was no longer making progress. His face was contorted, and white with exhaustion. He stared at them in a way that looked imploring. But when he actually saw them, he smiled. It was a ghastly smile, but it was definite. He shouted 'We'll make it.' Sandra saw, with shock, that he was naked. The tide had torn even his pants away.

The black man, too, had moved some feet closer to the buoy. If he had had the strength he would have saved himself at last. He twisted his head to them, though, and his face was agonised.

'Help me,' he said, softly. 'Help me *please*. I can't hold on no longer.'

'Hang on,' said Terry, urgently. 'Hang on, feller, just a second. We'll get you, mate, we'll save you. Just hang on.'

He started to pay the rope out over the stern, careful that it was well clear of the propellor. It flowed downtide towards Tony, who watched it coming. When it was near enough, he let go of the chain with his left hand and groped for it. His head went under, and his right hand slipped. He was pushed towards the gaping chasm, and Sandra gave a little scream. After five seconds he came up again, coughing water. He clawed his way, with both hands, slowly up the chain a foot or two. It was all he could make.

'Help me,' said the dangling black man. 'My arms. Oh help me, God.'

Oh Jesus, Jesus, Jesus, said Sandra to herself. She was on the verge of tears. Oh Tony, Tony, Tony, get that rope.

He did. It took him two more minutes, that felt more like a lifetime. He got the rope and began to wind it round his wrist, slowly, desperately slowly. Sandra and Terry were holding their end so hard it almost hurt. Just give them time to get him in, to get him safe.

'Keep holding, feller, please,' implored Terry. 'We'll get you, mate, I promise. You must keep holding.'

The black man couldn't. Abruptly, with a kind of high-pitched groan, he dropped from the top chain. He dropped across the lower one, which moved on the buoy-top with a metallic clank. Gripped by the tide, scrabbling for a handhold, he was pushed down the chain towards Tony. He stopped himself about two feet away.

On the boat, Sandra and Terry watched, completely helpless. They stood there in the sun and breeze, surrounded by the noise of the thumping diesel and the rushing tide.

Then Tony Gardiner began to move. With awful slowness he edged closer to the man. When they were touching, on the chain, he began to unwind the rope-end from his wrist. He worked it round the black man's shoulders, underneath his arms, then passed it round his wrist, slowly, terribly slowly, for two or three turns. The black man finally held it, as the rushing water banged their faces into each other repeatedly. Tony gave a strangled shout to the boat.

'Pull.'

They could do no other, although Sandra was in a trance of horror. Terry began hauling, and she took up the slack as it came round the Samson-post. They were tireder, and the work was even harder. Blood was weeping from her finger nails, and Terry's shirt was split from neck to waist. His wallet had fallen from his torn back pocket, and pound notes and photographs were scattered on the soaking deck. The blood was hammering in Sandra's ears and eyes and she was groaning constantly when they got the man over the stern. It must have taken ages.

When he had fallen to the deck, they looked for Tony. At first they thought he'd gone, but after a second or two his head burst through the surface, his face contorted and almost black. Sandra grabbed for the rope, and made to jump with it onto the stern. But it was still wound round the

76

black man, and in any case, as she moved, Terry pushed her hard and roughly across the boat.

'Get back!' he roared. Sandra screamed, and Terry began dragging at the rope, desperately, furiously. She looked over the stern, and saw Tony Gardiner let go. The chain slipped from his hands, and a small wave splashed almost merrily over his face. She screamed again, loudly, and Terry leapt to her side. Together they watched as Gardiner floated between the high, black bows, into the narrow, foaming cleft.

He clung there for long seconds, his white hands scrabbling at the weedy, tarry plating. Then he was pushed under by the tide, to be rolled and dragged along the bottom of the hulls until he sank.

ELEVEN

By the time it was all over, they had an escort. As Sandra turned away, stunned, from the hulks, she saw the lifeboat. It was coming across the tide at forty five degrees, its sides lined with anxious-looking men. There were other boats as well, inshore fishing boats, the ferry company's launch. As their motorboat dropped rapidly downtide towards the basin, she saw the gaggle of craft nose towards the sterns of the hulks. In case Tony Gardiner's body floated clear. To her disgust, she saw pleasure craft among them, crowded with excited holidaymakers, attracted by the activity.

On the journey back to the wharf, Sandra would have been in a coma, probably. But Terry, his face blank, set her to work. He put his arm round her shoulders and hugged her, once. 'Come on, kid,' he said, quietly. 'We're police. We're on a job. Get these poor bastards seen to.'

She stumbled into the fo'c'sle, past the silent boatman, and dragged out blankets and a piece of canvas. Terry was kneeling by the black, who seemed unconscious. As Sandra manhandled the white man as best she could, to wrap a blanket round him, Terry gave the other man the kiss of life. Within three minutes he was conscious again. They lifted him gently and wrapped him in blankets, also. Then Sandra flopped down, almost done. The blood from her hands had stained the blankets.

At the quayside there was a reception committee. There were three ambulances, about five patrol cars, and – oddly – a fire engine. Also, inevitably, there was the Press. She recognised, dully, David's flame-orange Metro. It was parked among a mass of cars, behind which was a crowd of people, being held back by the police. Rubberneckers, she thought. Sightseers. Oafs.

Suddenly, Sandra was filled with hatred and rage, mainly directed at David. You bastard, she thought, you awful, bloody bastard. A good man dead, a fantastic copper killed just doing his duty. And you're here, like a foul sort of vulture. It's disgusting. As she and Terry were helped ashore, after the two men in blankets had been lifted off by ambulance crew, David and a photographer tried to move forward. But they were jostled back, roughly, almost brutally. Clearly, Sandra's feelings were shared.

In fact, the general police reaction – voiced by the two officers who accompanied her and Terry in their ambulance to take the first details – was stronger than her own. It was rage, frustration, hatred and horror. For it was assumed, they all assumed, that the Press who had given them such a pasting over Mansoor, who had gone to town and done a total knife-job, would hardly care that some poor copper had sacrificed himself to save two men. They wouldn't give a damn. And one of them a black. The awful irony was lost on nobody.

It was utter nonsense, of course. The Press went absolutely crazy. Sam Renton pulled out all the stops – although he was on a hiding to nothing for that afternoon's editions – and Seawave interrupted programmes constantly, as they got more and more background. Interviews with the boatman, interviews with the families of the two boatyard workers who had been saved, interviews with neighbours of the dead policeman. By five fifteen television crews had arrived from all the nearby stations, and from ITN and BBC in London. Noor Allahi, if he'd ever been considered as newsworthy, was forgotten. This was the real thing. It was a journalist's dream.

Sandra and Terry were taken to hospital to be checked over, have their cuts cleaned and covered up, and treated for shock if necessary. By the time they got there Terry could hardly walk, having apparently injured his back in the mighty effort he'd put into hauling on the rope. Sandra was trembling with exhaustion, white-faced with depression. She couldn't get the picture from her mind, the picture of Tony Gardiner's face before he had slipped under. They were both put to bed and given sedatives. As she became unconscious, Sandra had a painfully vivid awareness that Terry had lost his best friend.

'Death of a Hero' was the obvious newspaper angle, and it was the one the popular papers took, with uncanny lack of differentiation. Sandra sat up in her hospital bed and read them one by one, with Maggie sitting at her side. When she'd put the last one down, her sister said: 'Well it's something, I suppose, Sandra. It's nice to know it was appreciated.'

Indeed, from the way the populars went on, Tony was one of the greatest heroes of all time. But it did not lift Sandra's depression, nor, when she spoke to her colleagues later, had it done much for them, either. There was a feeling of deep despair over the whole tragedy. The *Echo*, because it could only do a follow-up, having missed the main story because of edition times, did not manage to lift the cloud of hatred it was under. It had nothing new to add, so it was scanned and thrown aside. The Mohammed Mansoor debacle was still in all their minds.

Throughout the morning Terry and Sandra had many requests for interviews, which they turned down. There was a phone call from the *Echo*, which she refused to take, and half an hour later a sneak visit from David. A sister came into Sandra's room and told her there was a man outside who said he was sure she would see him, however many others she had refused. Sandra felt cold anger. 'Tell him to – Tell him to go away,' she said. 'Tell him I don't want to talk to him. Tell him I won't.'

She had many visitors – as did Terry – from her family and from the force. Brian turned up early that evening with an enormous bunch of flowers, and grapes and chocolates. He put his hand behind her head and kissed her gently on the mouth. Gently but proprietorially. 'Get well soon, chick,' he said. 'We've got a lot to do.'

Sandra was given time off to recuperate, and almost despite herself, she started going out with Brian. She was in a sort of daze, and she didn't really think about it, she didn't seem able to. The first night he took her to a very classy roadhouse in the country, and he was as tender and gentle as could be. They had cocktails, and a bottle of expensive wine, and lovely food. The lights were soft, and there was a small band playing romantic music in a corner. After they had eaten, they danced, and Brian held her cheek to his.

It all felt to Sandra as if she wasn't there, as if it was happening to someone else. She heard the music, watched the coloured ceiling lights, felt the arms around her and the face touching hers. But it was not real. She was in cotton wool. That night they went back to Brian's flat, but still she wasn't there, it didn't crack her consciousness. They went out every night from then, as he was working early shifts, and always ended up in bed. It was not a happy time.

David took to ringing every evening, and in the daytime as well. At night she was not in, and during the day she would not talk. Her mother, who had to answer the phone despite her leg, because Sandra wouldn't, did not like to lie. 'You ought to speak to him,' she told her daughter. 'It's not fair. Be honest, girl.'

Sandra couldn't. She could not talk, she did not dare. And as for being honest! God! One day he drove into the street and parked his car not far away from the house. Sandra's mother spotted it, and called Sandra to look, from behind the curtain. Sandra would not come, and after half an hour, David drove away.

She did not see him for something over a week.

Tony Gardiner's body was not found for days. As the tide had been running so fast, it was assumed that it had been taken out to sea, and possibly caught in the underwater obstructions off the coast. In fact it turned up several miles away, headless and appalling. When it had been identified, when Terry was on his feet once more, and Gardiner's widow was considered fit enough, a funeral and memorial service was held.

It was a big and sombre affair, and the weather played its part by being wet, cold and terrible. The media came down in force, with outside broadcast vans humming gently in the narrow streets round the cathedral, and thick black cables everywhere. There was a crowd of more than two thousand, and the police were there in hundreds.

Although Sandra was not religious, she found the ceremony inside the church almost unbearable. She and Terry were with the Gardiner family, and the tears and desolation of the widow recreated in Sandra a sense of loss that nearly overwhelmed her. During the Bishop's address a fixed vision came into her mind of the last seconds of Tony's life, as vivid and distorted as it had become in her dreams. There was a great weight in her chest, she found it hard to breathe. She was close to fainting.

The ceremony was very long. After the Bishop had spoken, there were addresses by other civic dignitaries, including the Chief Constable. At some moments Sandra achieved an almost trancelike state, the music and prayer washing over her. At one point she focussed on the massed faces of Tony's former colleagues, pale and rigid, many wet with tears. The emotion was all but palpable.

As the mass of people processed slowly outside to the huge, dripping graveyard, that emotion in the ranks of the police, closer to the surface than at any time since the disaster, received a powerful shock.

It was, of course, considered fitting that the saved men and their families were there, to pay their respects. One of them was black, and that was fair enough. It was an odd sight, in a way, the one black family, six or seven of them, in formal mourning clothes among the sea of white faces. But even the children were superb, correct and rigid, with their faces intent and shining in the rain. But when Kenny Baby Shaw and members of the race equality campaign were spotted, there was an almost tangible reaction from the force.

Sandra noticed them through a mist of tears. Gardiner's coffin was being prepared for lowering into its grave and she was standing with the family party, staring out across the tree-lined cemetery. The only one she recognised, at first, was Ahmed Rashid, and then, standing beside him, Peter Croxley. Then, with a sort of implosion in her stomach, she saw David. Beside him was a man she recognised from photographs as Shaw, and beside him a large, bearded black she guessed was 'Rastus'. There were others, Asian, white and black.

She glanced sideways at Terry, and saw that he had noticed them as well. His face, already drawn, had set into a harder line. It was incredible. It struck her as insulting, appalling, a deliberate affront. These people were always on the attack, were troublemakers, were constantly turning the knife. What were they doing here, to witness the burial of a brave – and no doubt to them despised – policeman? As for David . . . It was only a wonder, she thought savagely, that he had not brought Noor along. For a story.

In fact, it *had* been David's idea, and at first Kenny Baby Shaw had pooh-poohed it. He'd seen it as inappropriate, so soon after the Mansoor thing. But David, who had been almost constantly in touch with the REC since their first meeting in the Commercial Hotel, had argued strongly that Shaw was wrong, that it was a positive opportunity.

'It would be a terrific gesture,' he had said. 'It would show the police that despite everything, despite Noor Allahi, even, you recognised what they'd done. This young copper kills himself saving a black. You really ought to turn up, Kenny, you really ought to. To show your appreciation. To *prove* that you're not anti-police. When they do something good, for once, it shouldn't go unnoticed.'

Although he'd thought it would make a good story and picture, David had also been sincere. He'd had no idea just how deeply the *Echo* had wounded the police over Noor Allahi, aided and abetted by Kenny Baby's team. He'd had no idea just how little the *Echo*'s later tales of Tony's heroism had changed their attitude. He'd not associated Sandra's behaviour towards him with the case at all, just assumed she was in a state of shock or something. Ahmed and Croxley, who had become involved with the REC when Noor's ordeal had been made public, agreed with him.

'I think it's a good idea,' Ahmed had said. 'After all, this bloke did save that feller's life. And he gave up his own to do it. He gave him the rope and all.'

Riccard remained sceptical, but his arguments, for once, carried little weight. He said, merely, that the gesture would be misinterpreted, that the police would think they were being smart. The others could not see it, and half-suggested that he, Riccard, was being over-sensitive. Had he dared, David would have voiced what he truly thought: that Riccard resented that a policeman – and a white man at that – had been prepared to lose his life, and had become a hero, to save a black. In any case, despite Riccard, the idea took hold, became the subject of a genuine enthusiasm in the REC. And they turned up, in appropriate mourning, as a mark of real conciliation and respect. David's biggest mistake was to accompany them. The Press and the race campaign were already seen as one, unfriendly, entity. This confirmed it.

At the end of the day, when the crowds had dispersed and the official mourners had gone their separate ways, the police were full of it. It was generally agreed to have been a gross and calculated insult to the memory of a brave and selfless man. They were very bitter.

Two days later, Noor Allahi was rearrested.

TWELVE

The desperate thing, for Sandra, was that she seemed to have been the cause of it. She was back at work now, with only her split nails and sore fingertips to remind her physically of the tragedy when she picked things up carelessly, and she was back with Jackies One and Two in the filing room. The investigation into the murder of Yusuf Mansoor was theoretically back in top gear, and she had spent another couple of days in the caravan. Things down there were bad. The police attitude to the Asians had become much harder, and there had been reactions from the local population. Slogans had been scratched and painted on the caravan, and its tyres had twice been let down. The mildest slogan was 'Police Pigs Go Back to Sty.'

Jackie Two, who was well aware by now that Sandra knew Noor Allahi and presumably other Asians, deliberately goaded her when he was rearrested. For the suspicion this time was not that he had killed his father, but that he was not even related to him. Noor Allahi was being held as an illegal immigrant.

Sandra, when she had heard, had hardly been able to believe it. Whatever changes her feelings had gone through in the past few days she had assumed that once the science boys had cleared Allahi, that was that. The latest thing struck her as being plain vindictive, mad.

'The funny thing,' said Jackie Two, with quiet relish, 'is that it's all your doing, love. Well, not all, but you helped speed it up. Well done!'

Sandra looked to Jackie One for help, but she only shrugged. This was a private battle.

'Of course,' said Jackie Two, 'we'd have found out in the end that he's illegal, 'course we would. Like we've always told you, it's routine that gets there in the end. It never fails.'

She waved a hand airily at the table, covered now with an absolute mass of papers. Sandra remained doggedly silent.

'But I must admit you helped, though. That was the key, you knowing he was lying about his name. We'd come across that other name, but it hadn't clicked. It might have taken ages. Stroke of luck, eh Jack? You and Sandy meeting him in the corridor. Stroke of luck.'

Jackie One, put on the spot, nodded, as non-committally as possible.

'But he's not illegal,' said Sandra. 'It's nonsense, it's rubbish. I told you at the time, Jackie, when we met him. It's a religious thing, it's not significant.'

'Yeah, and you can tell *that* to the marines,' said Jackie Two. 'Religious thing my foot. If you'll pardon the expression, love, that's a load of balls.'

Sandra almost flared up.

'Well I've known him for years,' she said. 'I was at school with him. If he's here illegally, I'm a Chinaman.'

'Velly pleased to meet you,' said Jackie One. She was trying to take the steam out of things but it didn't help.

'Honestly,' said Jackie Two. 'You're a prize, you are Patterson. You're so naïve. You'd believe anything anyone told you, just so long as they were black. You're a real Paki-lover you are, aren't you?'

'Look,' said Sandra angrily. 'I'm not going to stand for this. Look. This is . . . it's –'

Jackie One took her arm. She spoke to Jackie Two.

'Give over, gal, give over. It's not on, that sort of talk, Jackie. Don't upset the girl.'

Jackie Two smirked.

'*Sorry*,' she said, with great exaggeration. 'I didn't mean to hurt your feelings, love. I'm *sure*.'

Jackie One called a smoke and tea break. But a few minutes later, when they were back at work, Jackie Two continued the attack.

'Anyway,' she said, as though carrying on a thought. 'We'll know soon enough this time. The Special Branch is in. They don't mess about.'

Sandra went cold. In the police mythology the Special Branch were the cream. The hardmen. Almost all the younger coppers had an urge to join them, which they usually kept a secret. In case they got laughed at for their presumption.

'His feet won't touch the ground,' said Jackie Two. 'They'll go through him like a dose of salts. His feet won't touch the ground.'

After a pause Sandra asked Jackie One: 'Why the Special Branch, Jackie? I thought they were only after criminals. You know, big ones, gangs and that.'

The younger woman giggled. Jackie One pushed back a strand of hair.

'Not necessarily,' she said. 'They do things that we don't get mixed up in as a rule. It's often like you said, but they handle all sorts. They'll be working with the immigration chaps on this. It's a Home Office job. They'll be down from London, I expect.'

'Down like a ton of bricks,' said Jackie Two, with satisfaction. 'His little black tootsies won't even touch the ground.'

Throughout headquarters, Sandra discovered later, the feeling was the same. She had lunch in the canteen with Brian and Terry, and a young constable called Dennis. Brian and Dennis were cockahoop.

'I hope they beat seven kinds of crap out of him, that's all,' said Dennis, a forkful of sausage hovering near his mouth. 'That's what the little git deserves. Seven separate kinds.'

'They will all right,' said Brian. 'They don't mess about, you know. He'll wish he'd never been born.'

'It's one in the eye for Ted Winter,' said Terry, sardonically. 'He's not a kid glove merchant, himself. If they nail something on miladdo he'll be sick.'

'Oh they'll be generous,' Brian laughed. 'They'll probably

'leave the pieces lying around for Ted to kick into the dustbin. They're not greedy men.'

Sandra, who was toying uncomfortably with steak pie, gave a nervous smile.

'They wouldn't really touch him, would they, though?' she said. 'Anyway, there's an immigration bod as well, isn't there? Or more than one?'

The three men looked at her, then at each other. Dennis said: 'Are you kidding, love? Not touch him? They'll –'

'Drop it, Den,' said Terry. 'Use your mind, chum, eh?'

Dennis frowned. He was puzzled. Brian spoke. His tone was jokey.

'Sandra's only young, you know,' he said. 'She's only a cadet, Dennis. You wouldn't like her to get the wrong impression, would you?'

The sense of chill she had felt in the filing room returned.

'They are a bit of a law unto themselves,' said Terry. 'But don't let it worry you, love. Nothing bad'll happen. And yes, you're right. The immigration men have been popping in and out. So I shouldn't worry too much.'

There was an uncomfortable silence. Then Brian said: 'It's good they got the little sod for something, though. It was a real sickener when they let him go.'

'Maybe they'll get him to confess he did it after all,' said Dennis. 'Stranger things have happened.'

'Well,' said Brian. 'He's still Number One, he's got to be. But what the hell? Who cares if he did it or not? Just so long as they can nail him this time.'

'How do you mean?' said Sandra.

'Oh come on, love,' said Brian. 'You weren't born yesterday. Just so long as they can chuck him out. Deport him. Send him back.'

Sandra stared.

'Then we'll be able to drop the murder stuff,' said Dennis. 'Let it fade away. Die the death. Just another Paki-bashing. This time fatal. Great big deal.'

'Anyone for tea or coffee?' said Terry. 'I'm going to the counter for me pud.'

Brian and Sandra kept well apart in the station, to stop tongues wagging, but after lunch he managed to have a word with her in the corridor. He tried to make a date for the evening, but she said no. She eyed him almost with alarm, with distaste. She said she had a date with Maggie that could not be put off. He grinned easily, unaware of her tension, and moved to put his arm round her. Sandra wriggled away, like lightning, too quickly.

'What's up with you, then?' he asked, surprised.

'We're in the station,' she said. 'For God's –'

An inspector walked around the corner of the corridor. Brian stiffened, Sandra blushed. They got an odd look as he passed, and Brian realised he had been stupid. Before he could carry on the persuasion, Sandra used the incident as an excuse to move away.

'I'll see you tomorrow,' she said, over her shoulder. 'I really am tied up tonight. Honest.'

As it turned out, she decided it would be an idea to visit Maggie. She ate her tea broodily, and fobbed off any conversation about work. Her parents were very circumspect, fearing to probe in case the upset over Tony's death came to the surface once more. Even her mother, who once had been quite blasé over death (from the professional point of view) had been rather shaken by her daughter's unspoken sense of misery after the drowning. When she had finished, Sandra made her announcement: she would go and have a chat with Mag.

David had not rung for a couple of days, and Sandra had been far too preoccupied to worry much about him. But as she walked out of the bottom of the road, towards the bus stop, the orange Metro drew up beside her. She looked around, in a sort of panic, but there was no escape. It was either cause a scene or capitulate. She opened the door and got in, quietly.

'Hello,' he said. 'Stranger.'

The first few minutes were terribly strained. Sandra did

not speak, and David clearly did not know how to begin. He drove slowly, going nowhere in particular.

He finally said: 'Can I take you somewhere? Sandra? Were you going anywhere I can take you?'

She looked at him. He concentrated on his driving, pretending not to notice. He looked tense, unhappy.

'My sister's,' she said. 'Mag. You can take me there if you like.'

'Fine,' he said. He gave a little, forced laugh. 'I thought you might be off to see your bloke,' he said.

Sandra recognised the ploy. He was fishing. She did not reply.

He speeded the car up, drove with more purpose. Nothing was said for a good long time. Then he said: 'Listen, Sandra, are you trying to tell me something? To say you've been avoiding me for the last couple of weeks is the understatement to end all understatements. What have I done wrong? Are you trying to get rid of me?'

They drew up at some traffic lights. He put his hand across and put it on her knee. He squeezed. He tried to take her hand, but she moved it, rapidly.

'What's up?' he said. 'What's going on? *Is* there another feller?'

'The lights,' she said thickly. 'They're green. For God's sake, David.'

There was a blast on a horn behind them. David slammed the Metro into bottom and shot off. He made the tyres scream at the next corner. At the end of Maggie's road he stopped the car. And switched the engine off.

'If you're trying to give me the bum's rush you've no chance,' he said. 'I'm not going. I'm your boyfriend, right, and I love you. Now: spit it out.'

Slowly, Sandra looked at him. His face was set, determined. But not pleading. She felt oddly reassured.

'Everyone said it couldn't last,' she said, softly. 'When I joined the police. It is difficult, Dave. I'm sorry. It's terrible.'

He smiled, rather sadly.

'Yeah,' he said. 'I'm sorry, Sandra, I don't like to put you on the spot. You've had a rough time, haven't you? Was he a mate, like, the one that died?'

Sandra's eyes filled with tears. She nodded. But even in the rush of emotion, she knew that she was lying, wallowing. Tony Gardiner hadn't been a mate, she'd hardly known him. But it was easier. She was sorry for herself, not him. But it was easier to use him this way. She nodded more, and a tear spilled over.

'Yeah,' she said. 'Sort of.'

David reached across and put his arm round her shoulder. At first her body stiffened, she started to resist. Then she relaxed. He held her for a short while like that. He did not try to kiss her.

'I've had to keep away, Dave,' she went on. 'It's been impossible. If they'd known, it would have been appalling. We're on opposite sides, Dave. It's a fence.'

'Yeah,' he said. 'I guessed you felt like that. It's been hard.'

'Why did you do it, Dave?' she said. 'Why did you turn up at the funeral like that? With that slimy bastard Shaw? I nearly died.'

'Why?' he said. 'We thought it was the right thing to do. It was a gesture. A mark of respect.'

Sandra sat up straight. She stared at him in amazement. He looked back, his arm stretched by her movement. He looked puzzled.

'It was,' he said. 'Honestly. Is that so hard to understand?'

'Good God,' said Sandra. 'If only you knew. They hate you for it, that's all. The lot of you.'

David thought of Riccard, and his argument. He changed the subject.

'This Noor Allahi thing,' he said. 'The rearrest. There's going to be trouble, Sandra, it's inevitable. They've gone doolalley tap. He's an innocent kid. There'll be hell to pay.'

Sandra stared out through the windscreen. Her sister's road was short and curved. Men in shirtsleeves were cleaning their cars in their drives. She felt hopeless.

'I've got to go to Maggie's, Dave,' she said. 'She's expecting me. I'm babysitting. I'd better go.'

He took his arm from around her shoulder and reached for the ignition key.

'It's a put-up job,' he said. 'You know that, don't you, Sandra? It's revenge. The cops and the Home Office. They've worked it out between them. To take the pressure off. They'll get Allahi if it's the last thing they do.'

She did not reply, so he started up the engine. He put the car into gear, but he did not move off.

'Can I take you out soon, Sandra?' he said. 'Please. I love you, d'you know that? Just say the word and I'll drop you off at Maggie's. I won't make another sound. Please.'

He eased out the clutch and they moved slowly towards the house. Sandra bit her lip.

'I don't know, Dave,' she said. 'I need more time.'

He pulled up. Through the front window she could see Maggie by the television. She hoped that she would not look too surprised to see her 'baby-sitter'. She felt a rush of longing to be with Dave. She leaned across and kissed his cheek.

'I'll see,' she said. 'I think so, Dave, I do. But I need more time.'

He moved his hand as if to grab her, then dropped it to his lap.

'Please,' he said.

He smiled a bent sort of smile.

'Did you notice?' he said, as she opened the door and started to get out.

'I haven't called you "old girl" once.'

His smile got odder still. She felt torn.

'Or a pig,' he added.

THIRTEEN

As soon as Maggie saw her sister she knew that something was up. She shoved the children out of the room, and sat her on the sofa.

'You look like you need a drink,' she said. 'Tea, coffee or gin?'

Sandra asked for tea, then changed her mind. Maggie called through the door to Roger that he was on children duty, and got the bottle out of the sideboard. She went out to the fridge and returned with an ice-tray and a big bottle of tonic.

'It's only slimline, love,' she said. 'Some of us have got to watch ourselves, you know.'

Sandra smiled, and poured herself a big one. She stretched her legs out and tried to relax. It wasn't easy.

'That was David, wasn't it?' said Maggie, half-casually. 'Why didn't you invite him in?'

'I dunno, Mag,' said Sandra. 'Too much trouble I expect. I told him you were waiting for me. Babysitter.'

'You're getting a right little liar in your old age,' said Maggie. 'Is it being in the police?'

She laughed, but Sandra didn't. She sipped her drink, her hand trembling slightly.

'Come on, lovely', said Maggie at last. 'What's the problem?'

It was hard, to begin with. The 'problem' was that there were too many problems. She didn't know where to start.

'I don't know where to start, Mag,' she said. 'I'm in a mess.'

'What kind of mess? David?'

'Not just him at that,' said Sandra, quietly.

'Ooh, you dirty cow,' said Maggie. 'Come on, give us all the lurid details. And don't cry all over me new suite!'

It came out gradually. Sandra told Maggie that she was sleeping with a colleague, that she didn't know if she still wanted to go with Dave, that the whole thing of police work was breaking her into pieces. She talked about the death of Tony Gardiner, the Noor Allahi thing, the nastiness of Jackie and the terrible times at the caravan. By the time she'd reached the bottom of her second glass she was sunk in gloom.

'Gawd, gal,' said Maggie. 'This is meant to cheer you up, you know. Crying on your sister's shoulder.'

'I wish I could,' said Sandra. 'I can't even cry properly any more. I squeezed a few out in the car just now and it was all a great big act. I'd love a real good bawl. I'm so tensed up.'

'There's nothing for it, then,' said Maggie. 'We'll have to get you pissed. I wouldn't mind myself, either, come to that.'

She insisted, laughingly, that they couldn't get drunk at home, because it wouldn't be respectable. She went and had a word with the long-suffering Roger, who put his face round the door and grinned at Sandra. He was a big, friendly man.

'You're a terrible influence on my wife,' he said. 'She used to be such a quiet little thing till she met you. When we going to start those lessons up again, you haven't had a drive for yonks? We're on our holidays in a couple of weeks, how about after that?' He disappeared without waiting for a reply.

Sandra and Maggie walked to a quiet pub nearby, because Maggie was expecting to drink far too much for driving on. They carried on on double gin and tonics, but it was ages before they became giggly. When they did, things got better.

'Is he good-looking?' asked Maggie. 'This Brian bloke? Ooh. I'm jealous really, gal. I could use a great big hunk of copper!'

'Oh he's that all right,' said Sandra. 'He makes poor

David look like the weed he is. He's a great big blond thing with hair all down his back!'

But sombre flashes kept intruding.

'Do you love him, gal?' said Maggie.

'No,' said Sandra. 'That's the trouble. I think I still love Dave.'

And later.

'I think I'm afraid of him really, Mag. He's got a vicious streak. I'm sure of it. The way he acts at work, too. He's divorced, Brian. They don't let him see his kids. I sometimes think I don't like him much. Oh Jesus.'

She talked a lot about Noor Allahi, which had the tipsy Margaret laughing aloud. She kept wanting to know why Sandra was so bothered.

'You're not like that about them, are you?' she said. 'He's just some little black lad that probably killed his dad.'

Sandra giggled.

'No,' she said. 'But David might be. He's as thick as thieves with that equality lot. It's strange.'

It was. She hadn't pondered it before. She had a sudden vague memory of how he'd been with that Indian waiter once. But she cared over Noor, as well. Why, exactly? It seemed somehow very important that she should answer Maggie's question, but she was drunk. It was all too much for her.

'I went to school with him,' she said. 'It just seems daft, that's all.'

By closing time they were fairly legless and very jolly. She kipped down in the spare bed, and had the best night's sleep she'd had for ages. The next morning she had a cracking headache and a sick feeling in her stomach, but it had been well worth it. She felt relaxed, refreshed. Nothing had changed, but she felt much more able to face things.

It didn't last for long once she'd got to work, though. And the sick feeling in her stomach increased significantly.

For at seven o'clock that morning, she was told by a watchful Jackie Two, Noor Allahi had confessed.

He *was* an illegal immigrant.

       *   *   *

At the offices of the REC, the news brought first disbelief, then anger, then a kind of savage fury. By the time David got there, in the afternoon, the atmosphere had modified once more. It was determined, and bitter, but with a new, and definite, sense of purpose. Something had to happen, and it had a focal point. He went into the smoke-filled room where the talk was going on. Despite his position as a reporter, it was accepted now, almost totally, that he was one of them.

That acceptance had taken a lot of time and effort. Riccard had been the main stumbling block, and if David had not so admired the man, he would perhaps have thought at first that his attitude was racist. He still, in fact, had flashes of secret doubt. Riccard, basically, trusted very few whites indeed, and he trusted journalists least of all. He was used to being stereotyped, and he was used to being attacked. He thought the media superficial, tawdry, hysterical and malevolent.

'Listen,' he had said. 'The Press and radio and television in this country is either controlled by the Government, or in the hands of capitalists, right? They're openly anti-black and racist, and if you can't see that, you're blind. It's a plot.'

On facts, and he had plenty, Riccard could not be faulted. And in any case, David knew he was on dicey ground. He half agreed, for God's sake, and every time there was any major trouble, riots and so forth, the general Press coverage made him wild. But it was not so much a 'plot', he insisted, as Riccard thought. It was ignorance, arrogance, stupidity, greed. Journalists were people, just like anyone else, and they lived in a white-dominated, white majority country. They needed education, and they resisted it. But *he* should not be mistrusted out of hand, because he was a journalist. That was irrational, like mistrusting a black because he was black.

There were several arguments, and they were hard work and rather frightening. Riccard was a formidable opponent, and David had to think, and think hard, about his real motives. But on the *Echo*'s coverage of the Noor Allahi case at least, from the very start, there could be little argument. And David, even Riccard was bound to concede, had got it off the ground. After a time, he laid off David, but he rarely spoke to him, and never smiled. David was, however, accepted by the group.

Now, on the afternoon of the 'confession,' David entered a meeting of the full inner circle of the REC. There were Shaw and Riccard in the room, along with Shaw's wife Sara, Ahmed and Peter Croxley. About five other members lounged around.

'Hi,' he said. 'I've just heard on Seawave. I've been off. It's incredible. I honestly think they've gone mad this time, it's extraordinary.'

'What did Seawave say?' asked Shaw. 'It didn't occur to us to listen.'

David sat down.

'Not a lot,' he said. 'It's too early yet. They just read a police statement that Mohammed Mansoor, alias Noor Allahi, had signed a statement to the effect that he'd come in illegally. The murdered man was his uncle. End of story.'

'Jesus Christ,' said Sara. 'No denial? No "allegation" or nothing?'

'Oh come on, Sara,' said David. 'Be reasonable. If the police put that statement out, there's nothing anyone can do except report it. You can't just say they're liars. It's what happens now that counts. It's what we do next. It's up to us.'

'I still can't believe it,' said Ahmed. 'If this had happened in Russia, to a dissident, everyone would have shook their heads. Another atrocity. Another innocent person slammed in jail on a trumped-up charge. But this is England. Now. No outcry.'

Riccard grunted.

'Brainwashing,' he said. 'Who's going to believe the good old British Home Office behave like the Kremlin? They're just the same, brother. Fascists, just the same. Begum, Mehta, Azad; Kelly, Towers, Peach; Brixton, Toxteth, Southall. It's all the same old game.'

David nodded.

'It's an act of revenge,' he said. 'It's blatant. The cops'll never find the murderer, because they're never going to try. They arrested Noor Allahi and they made themselves look stupid. This is their revenge.'

'I can't stop thinking of his mother,' said Sara. 'This time we must help. This time we know, so there's no excuse. God knows what she must be going through. Again.'

Riccard said: 'This time we've got to act on more than just his mother, though. We've got to make it big. We've got to get a mass movement going.'

Kenny Baby Shaw nodded, but he sounded a note of caution.

'There's a danger in "mass movements",' he said. 'We've seen it too often before. Things get distorted. Everyone takes sides. The Press doesn't help, David, as I'm sure you'll agree.'

Sara said: 'We'll have to make it formal. Get up a petition. Start a separate defence committee. The Noor Allahi Committee of Defence. Keep it cool.'

The talk went on for ages, and for some of them it was costly, those who'd left their work when the REC solicitor monitoring the case had told Shaw of the 'confession'. By mid-evening, though, they had a plan. They would form a committee, they would approach all the Asian organisations in the town, and speak to the minority community leaders, even those who felt the REC was a Marxist-orientated and too-strident pressure group. They'd set up a joint petition, buy poster space and advertising space, and David would do his best to make sure that everything got publicity. As soon as they had sufficient support they would march. They would keep marching, as well, getting bigger and bigger every time, they hoped. They would have to see.

David drove home to his flat excited and well pleased. His position was a delicate one, because he had no intention of letting his full involvement with the REC be known to anyone, and he was fully aware that in terms of professional ethics he was on a very sticky wicket. But some things, he thought, were too important to be squeamish over.

He thought of Sandra, also, before he went to sleep, but there was no excitement there. The rift was widening, and this could only make it worse. He tried to fantasise for a while, but there was no pleasure in it. Knowing his luck he'd probably meet her on the march, the very first one. And it would be a disaster.

In the event they did meet, and it was. It was a disaster for both of them.

FOURTEEN

To David's genuine surprise, the *Echo* took a firm – and positive – line on the rearrest and confession of Noor Allahi, although as before it was apparently seen as a dead letter by the rest of the Press, and even local radio. After Seawave's first, brief bulletin, the subject was dropped. But in the *Echo* next day there was a remarkably fierce leader.

It did not dispute the facts as stated by the police, of course. If they said Noor Allahi had confessed, then clearly he had done so, no question. But it questioned the ethics of his rearrest, and what it referred to as the 'possible harrassment' of a young man, and his undoubtedly innocent family, who had suffered a great deal. What's more, the leader, while allowing the right of the Home Office and police to act as they had done, wondered if it did not at least smack of unfair treatment. It could not happen to a white, because the immigration laws were not aimed at whites. But in a 'civilised society that is proud of that epithet, should it have been allowed to happen to anyone, whatever his class, creed or colour?'

Considering that the editor had written it, it seemed incredible. David, who read it sitting at the newsdesk, was amazed.

'Hell, Sam,' he said. 'Have you read this? Old Johnson's flipped his tank. It sounds like Kenny Baby Shaw!'

Renton had read it. He laughed.

'Yes,' he said. 'Wonders never cease. That'll take the "capitalist Press" wind out of Kenny Baby's sails. And the black bomber's.'

'It's not going to chuff the fuzz that much, either!' said

David. 'It's unprecedented. The *Echo* just doesn't talk like that. Old Johnson's right of Genghis Khan.'

'I think he was a bit brassed off over the way they reacted to the earlier Mansoor stuff,' said Renton. 'The Chief Constable blasted him like mad. Said he was "siding with a criminal". Johnson might be a Tory, but he's straight, I'll give him that. The police claiming we're anti just because we catch them up to no good and have the temerity to print it is *not* his cup of tea. He's honest and he expects them to be.'

He lit a Gauloise and did his deep-draw routine.

'Anyway,' he said. 'He thinks it's all down to the Special Branch coming in. And the Home Office. He doesn't like immigrants, even if they're government officials from the Smoke! Noor Allahi's local. He's got to be looked after!'

As the Noor Allahi Committee of Defence got going with its protests, however, Renton's – and the *Echo*'s – attitudes returned to more familiar lines. The committee made a fair amount of noise, and the petition grew quite rapidly, so it had to be reported; it was a not-bad local story. But David – subtly – tried to push it hard, and in a direction Renton would not tolerate. It led to frequent friction.

'But everyone knows he's not illegal,' said David, at one point. 'It's obvious.'

Sam exploded.

'Listen, you prat,' he said furiously. 'You sound just like the REC. Drop it, mate. We're journalists, not PRs for Kenny Shaw.'

David was taken aback, because he thought his cover was good. That was too near the mark for comfort.

'Well, all right, I take your point,' he said. 'Nobody knows for sure. But the odds are . . . well, Shaw and Co are pretty sure. And you must admit the police's record on this case isn't that hot.'

'Look, pal,' said Renton. 'The police's record doesn't matter. It's facts that count. And when that leftist pillock Shaw and his moody marxist mate say they *know* Allahi's not illegal, it gets right up everybody's nose. Including mine. And I won't have you trying to push it in the *Echo*.'

'So we'll let them break the law and behave like fascist thugs without batting an eyelid,' said David. 'Great.'

'Balls.' Renton was scornful. 'You know that's rubbish, so knock it off. And knock off using bloody ridiculous words like fascist to describe the local policemen, it just makes *you* look daft. You can be as anti-police as you like in private, Tanner, but I'm not putting up with it in here. We'll cover everything, just like we have so far, as fairly and as accurately as we can. If the cops step out of line, so be it, we'll have 'em. And if Shaw and Rastus cock it up with their corrosive "fascism" crap, fair enough again. We'll report that as well.'

David was silent. Sam Renton went on.

'Disbelief is corrosive,' he said. 'Wild, unsubstantiated allegations are corrosive. Kenny Baby Shaw and Rastus are politicos. They're not interested in Allahi, they want to cause a stink. They're Marxists. They want to put the police on the spot. They're bent.'

David shook his head.

'No,' he said. 'I've spoken to them, Sam. They're genuine. They're sincere. The Marxist demon line's just rubbish. A handy label to smear them with. Honestly.'

Renton didn't argue, somewhat to Dave's surprise.

'Maybe,' he said. 'But if they're not bent, they're stupid. This sort of thing'll get them nothing but reaction. If they're blinded by emotion, fair enough. But they'd better not act surprised if everybody else gets blinded too – and the emotion's aimed at them. It'll blow up on them, flower, you mark my words, they'll put the world against them. The respectable world, the one that counts. See what Tory Johnson says then . . .'

In a room at Bentham remand centre, many miles outside the city, Noor Allahi sat across the table from an immigration official and stared at him in fear and disbelief. The man had explained it slowly, not without contempt at Noor's lack of fluent English, and had gone through it all twice. Two uniformed men flanked the boy, and the officer in charge of his wing, Mr Whitehead, stood nearby.

'Do you understand?' asked Whitehead. 'Is that quite clear now? You will be returned to Pakistan, probably in about four weeks, at a date yet to be fixed upon. The Home Office have decreed that you must be deported.'

'But my Mama,' Allahi stammered. 'My brother and my sister.'

The immigration official tutted impatiently.

'For God's sake, lad,' he said. 'I've told you twice already. We've got nothing against your mother and the children. They can stay. It's you that's going. You're going home.'

Allahi did not speak. He could not believe his ears. He could not believe that his mother, who could hardly even understand the language, who was lost and utterly alone, could be treated like this. How would she live? How would she survive? What of the babies?

The immigration official stood up.

'Right,' he said. 'I'm glad that's clear.'

Noor Allahi started to cry.

'It is false,' he said. 'It is not true. They made me sign that paper. I am right to be here. They made me sign.'

The men in uniform stared blankly ahead. The immigration official looked at Allahi in distaste.

'Don't give me that,' he said. 'You're pitiful, do you know that? You're absolutely bloody pitiful.'

As he left with the officer in charge he smiled.

'I don't envy you your job, Mr Whitehead,' he said pleasantly. 'It will be a relief to get back to London.'

On the day of the first big march, the REC had known of the decision to deport for half a week, and it had given their publicity and support extra momentum. As the marchers gathered, it became apparent that as well as several hundred Asians, there was more than just a smattering of whites. The implications of a boy who had come to England – illegally or otherwise – at the age of only ten or twelve being sent back to a country where he had no friends or close relatives, were beginning to stir some consciences. Not a vast number, and not official ones. But some. The plight of Mrs Mansoor and the children was also widely known. David had done another interview, and it had raised some heartrending possibilities.

Sandra was at headquarters early on the day, and she was involved in some of the logistical planning. She had been placed with the traffic unit for the past two weeks, and they had been given the task of co-ordinating the march control. Trouble was half expected, because it was not only the liberal conscience that had been stirred. The National Front and other fringe rightist groups had been muttering recently. Hindley Lane End had had a spate of window-smashings and street attacks on lone Asians, seen by the police – although they denied a racial motive in public – as responses to the attacks on the information caravan and the 'leftie bletherings' of the *Echo*. A vast contingent of police were to be deployed on the route, and the atmosphere in the station was one of excitement.

Sandra, however, was too preoccupied and unhappy to take much interest in the minimal tasks that had been assigned to her. Her affair with Brian, which had started oddly and had never brought her much but confusion and a vague feeling of unease, was deteriorating fairly rapidly. What was worse, perhaps, was that David, she assumed, had now ducked out for good. He had telephoned a few times, but he'd never sounded madly upset when she had told him she still wanted more time to sort things out. She thought he could not be interested anymore – and why should he be, after all? – and it increased her loneliness. She did not know, of course, just how closely he was bound up in the Allahi thing, and how it largely filled his mind.

The trouble with Brian was that he was getting serious, and he was getting very heavy with it. Sandra did not love him, she knew well, but he desperately wanted her to. She did not think he loved her, either, but he had a need to dominate, to control. He was very possessive, jealous even, and he kept trying to bring in rules and regulations about her behaviour, and even thoughts, that she could not stand. He had an attitude to 'morality', for instance, that she thought fundamentalist, but which he saw as being fundamental to a policeman's superior position as a guardian of society. He considered many quite ordinary people as 'scum' – for having long hair, say, or wearing 'sloppy' clothes – and thought that anyone who broke a law, however unimportant, had forfeited their right to any consideration as citizens of a 'decent' world. The police, therefore, could do no wrong, ever: they were the interpreters and upholders of the faith.

On 'bad language', as well, they had differences. Sandra swore quite a lot, she always had done, it was considered normal in her family. But Brian did not like it. He 'did not like to hear a woman swear'. He said it demeaned her, brought her down. Sandra had said once, in reply, that this was bullshit, and he had smacked her in the face, hard. She was a tough girl, and not that small, and normally she would have gone to town on any man who had done a thing like that. But for the first time in her life she was helpless. Brian was big, and strong, and had a streak of naked ruthlessness he was quite prepared to use against her. He held her wrists as she had raged, and smiled at her, a mocking, hateful smile. She was in his power, and she hated it. She despised him for it, too.

Brian was even jealous of her friendship with Terry, which annoyed her almost most of all. She really liked Terry enormously now, and they both felt bonded by the tragedy they'd shared. But Brian did not like them to go out together, on police work, and often made snide remarks. Terry took them easily, and went on with her as matily as ever, but Sandra seethed. Some evenings they had rows about it, and about his possessiveness in general, but he always dominated physically. He sometimes held her mouth closed with his hand until she gave up trying to argue. She felt helpless, then, a victim of brute strength.

It was not bad enough to make her try and escape, not yet in any case. She did not quite know how to, was the trouble.

But she felt frightened, desperate, when he tried to make her say she loved him. She always hedged it, but he tried always to insist. In a way, she felt sorry for him. She knew deep down that he was desperate, too, and probably unhappy to a depth she could not dream of. She regretted, bitterly, their entanglement.

The march started off at the incidents caravan at Hindley Lane End, and was routed fairly directly, via wide commercial streets, from the docks to the town centre, avoiding as far as possible the holiday haunts. It was a dull day, so plenty of people stopped to stare, people who might otherwise have been on the seafront. The marchers chanted from time to time, but they got little response from most of the onlookers. Visitors to the town tended not to read the local paper, so many of them didn't even know what it was all about. The banners, without basic knowledge, did not tell a lot: Free Noor Allahi. Fight Home Office Racism. End Deport Threat Now.

Sandra was stationed on the last stretch of the march, where it was due to go along Gibbs Street, a wide, not very busy road that led into the city centre proper. The number of police involved amazed her. Although she had helped sort out the lists, and she knew how many men and women were out, from every police station, in the flesh they looked extraordinary. It had been estimated that there were about five hundred marchers, and in Gibbs Street alone it looked as though the force outnumbered them.

The rightists had not sought permission for a counter march, and for the first mile or so it appeared that they were keeping a low profile. There was a bit of jeering every now and then, and a few rotten tomatoes and eggs had been hurled at the border of Hindley Lane End and the next district, which was the city's generally accepted 'stronghold' of the right. But all in all it had gone quite quietly.

There were police marching with the column, as well as lining the route, and as it turned and straggled slowly into Gibbs Street and towards her, Sandra saw that Brian was near the front. She also noticed, just ahead of the column, walking backwards some of the time while photographs were taken, a contingent of the Press. David was among them, and a Seawave man she knew as Alan Proctor. There were a couple of others she did not know, but very few all told. The nationals and the television were still not interested.

As the marchers came nearer, the whole atmosphere began to change. It was hard to follow, at first, but things quickly became clearer. The neo-fascists had decided to attack.

As far as Sandra could work out, there must have been a gang of them hiding up a sidestreet. At the point where the first horde broke through, there were quite a few ordinary people on the pavement, craning to see over the heads of the police. This, she imagined, must have prevented her colleagues from noticing what was building up.

At first it looked a minor incident, but the situation broke down with shocking speed. The crowd at the roadside surged, there was a burst of shouting, and a gang of white youths flooded into the road, towards the marching column. They were yelling, screaming almost, and although she could not catch the words, Sandra got the gist. It was racial abuse, and obscene at that. The marchers kept straight on, trying not to look. For a few moments the youths merely stood there, screaming and yelling. No missiles were thrown.

Sandra felt her stomach churning, and wondered why her colleagues had not made a move to round them up and cut them off. Within a few seconds, though, everything was confusion. After that it was impossible to work anything out rationally.

With extraordinary speed, two or three more breaches appeared in the wall of onlookers and police. A howling mob of thugs came rushing out from every direction, and this time they were throwing things. Rocks, bricks and bottles showered through the air, then the youths hurled themselves into the marching column. Sandra felt amazing pressure behind her, and the policeman standing next to her grabbed her arm. But it was too late. She was knocked sprawling into the road.

For several minutes, there was total chaos. The holiday-makers and passers-by got mixed up in the fray, lost and screaming children ran about in panic, and the air was filled with whistles, shouts and cries. Sandra, bruised and shaken, picked herself up from the road, dusted off her knees automatically, and ran for the affray. Every time she came face to face with a civilian she shouted 'Get away, get away. Go back. It's dangerous.'

The column tried to hold, but by the time she got there, the fight was fast and furious. She did not have time to take it all in, it was too confusing. She only saw some cameos, like movie film seen from the corner of the eye. She was giddy, in any case, with panic and excitement, the adrenalin was pumping in her veins. She was shocked and terrified.

When one of the cameos became clear before her eyes, she rushed towards it. It was a probationer constable she recognised, nineteen years old and frightened, fighting off three skinheads who were trying to tear an Asian girl of twelve or so out of his arms. Sandra shattered this cameo with the force of her arrival. She grabbed one of the skinheads by the upper arms and butted him so hard his nose burst. She also almost knocked herself out, and she staggered forward over the fallen thug, trying to keep her balance as her shoe sank in his stomach. Then she fell.

Minutes later, it was over. The thugs, triumphant or hurt and bleeding, ran whooping from the fray. The marchers, some of them quite badly hurt, several of them lying on the ground, tried to gather themselves together. They were an awful sight, torn and shaken, surrounded now by anxious, frightened passers-by who were being shooed and pushed at by the police. On one side of the road, by a van that had sirened its way urgently along Gibbs Road, was a knot of shouting Asians, surrounded by police. A superintendent was calling through an electric megaphone, ordering the marchers to disperse.

As Sandra stood there, drained and horrified, she saw

David coming towards her. Brian was beside her, too. He had sought her out and he was trembling with what seemed like exhaustion and elation, panting heavily.

David had a cut above his eye that was blackening rapidly into a monstrous bruise. He was shaking also. And white with fury.

He ignored Brian and spoke directly to her. He almost spat the words.

'You lousy fascist bitch,' he said. 'I hope you're satisfied. I won't be calling any more, Miss Patterson, I wouldn't be seen dead with you. You can go and stuff yourself.'

He turned on his heel. Sandra flinched, expecting Brian to jump on him. But he was looking at her, his face darkening with rage.

'What did that mean?' he said. 'Have you been tricking me, you cow? Have you been two-timing me?'

Oh God, thought Sandra. Oh my Jesus God.

FIFTEEN

There was no time for anything more to be said. There was the twin-tone blaring of ambulance sirens, and crowds to be parted, sorted out, comforted, dispersed. The police regrouped, and Brian and Sandra had to separate. Despite official exhortation, those marchers who were able insisted that the demo carry on. Most of the banners had gone, many of the marchers had torn clothes and bloody faces, several of them had to be helped along. There was no more chanting, no more friendliness or jollity. It was a stony, silent and impressive affair.

Back at headquarters, Sandra was cornered in the lavatories by Jackie Two. She was sickened by the whole affair and Jackie's taunting nastiness made her want to scream. She tried to close her ears, but the nagging, jeering voice bit home. Jackie's view was that the blacks had had it coming to them, and they'd think better of it before they marched again. She thought it was a scandal that the police had to appear to be siding with them, and she was glad the youths had run amuck. She didn't agree with no National Front, she said smugly, but you had to admit – they had a point.

There was no way, of course, that Sandra could avoid the night of reckoning. Brian was not off till late, but he spoke to her on an internal phone and made a date to meet her at nine-thirty, at the corner near her house. She did not argue, there was no point. In a way she was relieved. Something was coming into the open at last, for better or for worse. The lying had to stop.

It was for the worse, though, definitely for the worse.

Brian picked her up without a word and drove straight back to his flat. He was not going for the rational touch, in a pub, surrounded by a buffer of people to save her from his rage. He wanted the meeting on his terms, and his alone. Sandra's mouth was dry as she climbed the stairs behind him.

Brian closed the door and took his uniform jacket off. Sandra was wearing a light casual jacket, and she kept it on. She went and stood in the living room, waiting for him, while he went into the lavatory. She looked at the pictures on the wall, his children at the zoo, his wife and children with him in Ibiza, his children standing looking at the camera solemnly, dwarfed by the driving wheels of a vast steam locomotive. She put her hand out, held the back of the sofa. She was frightened.

Brian walked into the room purposefully, and stood in front of her. His face was grim.

'Well?' he said. 'What did that chap mean? That reporter chap?'

'I . . . I don't really know,' said Sandra, falteringly. 'I think maybe –'

Brian slapped her face, hard. His colour rose and the pupils of his eyes enlarged.

'Bitch,' he said. 'Don't mess about with me. I want to know the truth. Now.'

Sandra's face stung, but she felt no anger rising.

'I used to go out with him,' she said. 'That's all. He was my boyfriend.'

'He's a Pressman,' said Brian. 'He works on the *Echo*. He's been hounding us.'

He appeared genuinely surprised, as if the idea was too difficult to grasp, a police-girl and a newspaper reporter.

'Yes,' said Sandra. 'That's why we broke up. It was hopeless. It just couldn't work. But it took some time, that's all. We'd been going out for years.'

Brian moved his head from side to side, slowly.

'Crazy,' he said. 'I can't believe you'd go with scum like that. It's impossible.'

Irrationally, Sandra became annoyed.

'He's not scum,' she said. 'He's a very nice man. He's got some qualities that . . . he's got compassion. He cares for people.'

A look of contempt was large on Brian's face.

'A bloody ninny,' he said. 'Leftist scum. He's the sort that's destroyed the moral fibre of this country.'

Sandra said nothing. She was almost bored. She looked at Brian's handsome, rigid face and wondered how she could ever have fancied him. He reminded her of an animal. He was stupid, utterly without brain. He nauseated her.

Suddenly his eyes narrowed.

'What was that about not calling on you, then?' he demanded. 'About not being seen dead with you? Eh, tell me that. Tell me that, eh.'

'He's been trying to get me to change my mind,' said Sandra, tiredly. 'He's been ringing me up. He thinks there's still a chance for us.'

'What?' said Brian. His voice had altered. There was a warning note in it. 'How long's it been then? Since you packed up? How long before you fell in love with me?'

Sandra said recklessly: 'Not long. Not even after, as it happens. I was going with the both of you if you must know. And I *don't* love –'

She never finished the sentence. Brian gave a sort of roar and grabbed her by the throat. In a state of pure shock she felt her feet rise from the ground and her legs fly round in an arc. There was a searing pain as they banged into the television set, then her body flew across the room and crashed into the dining table. She ended up under it, with her mouth jammed against the hard square leg, bleeding from a torn bottom lip.

As quickly as it started, it was over. As Sandra stared at him – too shocked and dazed to even be afraid – Brian's face changed. It was staring, maddened, blinded – then it crumpled. He covered it with his hands and dropped onto his knees. When he finally spoke, his voice was broken.

112

'Forgive me, Sandra, please forgive me,' he said. 'Oh God, my love, I'm sorry. I just can't stand it any more. I just can't bear it.'

In her pain, Sandra was madly calm. Everything was finished now, she knew. Everything was past. Inside her mind she smiled, genuinely amused. *You* can't bear it, she thought. Jesus, Mister! If you only knew . . .

She lay there motionless for quite a time, in case the ordeal was, in fact, not over. She wondered whether she should make a move, if Brian would just let her go. When she did stand up, it was obvious that he would. He got to his own feet, almost formally, politely, and said: 'I suppose you'd better go. We'll talk about it later. I suppose you'd better go.'

It did not seem to occur to him that he had done anything wrong. That Sandra could, God spare the mark, go to the police. He did not seem to notice, when he turned the hall light on to let her out, that her face was marked with fingers, her lip split and swollen, and her throat an angry red. He did not even seem to notice that it was odd that she turned down the offer of a lift, although she had a long walk home in the dark. He said goodnight, and nodded dazedly, and closed the door.

Sandra stood in the road, drawing in great breaths of cold sea air. She wondered what to do. She couldn't go home like this, impossible. And Maggie was away on holiday. She didn't know what to do.

By the time she got to David's flat, reaction was beginning to set in. As she approached the street door it opened, and she jumped like a cat. She slipped into a shadow as a man came out. It was Peter Croxley. But she did not call out. She waited until he had walked down the deserted street, his heels sounding strangely loud.

Assuming that David was now alone, and not daring to ring the bell in case he came to the door and refused to let her in, she used her own key. She did so quietly, and almost

113

crept up the carpeted staircase. She was panting slightly when she reached David's door and opened it.

As she did so the reaction set in with a vengeance. Sandra, her hand still on the knob, began to shake, quite violently. David was not alone. Ahmed Rashid was with him.

Even in her state, Sandra found the sight a strange one. David had a bandage on his head and a huge weal down his right cheek. Ahmed had one hand done up in bandage and a glaring red and black bruise around his eye. She was nuttily conscious that they must make a great trio!

David stood up from his chair angrily. Ahmed just looked puzzled by her presence.

'What do you want?' David demanded. 'You're not welcome here, pig.'

Ahmed stood up. He put a hand out and touched David's arm.

'Come on, David, come on, man,' he said. 'The lady's not well. Sit down, love, before you fall down.'

Sandra moved forward. Her knees were trembling wildly.

'She's a pig,' said David. 'Why don't you sod off, Sandra? Why don't you just go home?'

Ahmed helped her to a chair.

'David,' he said, embarrassed. 'Drop it, man. Not all the police were bad today. Some of them got hurt on our behalf.'

'Yeah,' said David, moodily. 'But I bet our Sandra didn't, did you, love? I bet I know which side *you* were on.'

Sandra felt exhausted. Much too tired to argue, or get angry. Ahmed offered her a glass, and waved a half-bottle of whisky at it. She smiled and nodded and he poured her out a slug. She sipped it and it stung her mouth. But it was like nectar. She took a bigger drop. It was wonderful.

David sensed that the steam was going out of things. He said belligerently: 'Go on, then, how did you get that face? And what the hell do you mean, coming round here like this? I told you we were finished.'

Ahmed looked from one to the other of them slightly shocked. That David knew Sandra had clearly been news to

him. That she was his girlfriend – and her in the force . . .
He concentrated hard.

The whisky was warm in Sandra. She was half-hysterical,
deep inside. She felt like bursting into tears. Or giggles. She
said mockingly: 'Aren't you being rather racist, David?'

Her voice was terrible. Shaky with suppressed reaction,
and hoarse where Brian's hands had squeezed her windpipe.

David had sat down again.

'What are you on about?' he said. 'We've been sitting
here, you might like to know, making out a formal
complaint about the police. They're the racists, Patterson.
They let the fascists in, deliberately, and they helped them
in the fight. What do you mean, *I'm* being racist?'

'If a fascist didn't do this to my face, a marcher must have,
surely?' she said, still half-hysterically. 'I'm just amazed that
you could think a Pakistani could have hit a woman, that's
all. I thought they were above that sort of thing. I thought
all blacks were angels in your book.'

'You snide bitch,' he said. 'Why don't you piss off.'

Sandra took a large swallow of Scotch.

'If you must know,' she said, 'a policeman did all this. If
you were as observant as you think you are, you'd have
noticed that I didn't have it at the march. When you said
your charming little piece to me, remember?'

'A policeman?' said Ahmed. 'What do you mean?'

Sandra could not speak. She had her teeth clenched hard
together. She just shook her head from side to side.

'Good God,' said David. His whole attitude was changing
before her eyes. 'A copper? You mean a copper beat you
up?'

Sandra said in a strangled voice: 'That's what I said, isn't
it? That's what I said.'

'Why, though?' asked Ahmed. 'Why should a policeman
beat you up? What had you done?'

But David was ecstatic.

'I'll have to go in early', he said. 'I'll have to rewrite my
overnight piece. Jesus, what a story! My God, love, will you
bring charges? Will you do him for assault?'

Sandra could not believe it. A *story*? David thought it was a good *story*?

Ahmed tried to cover for his friend.

'But why?' he repeated. 'Why, Sandra, why?'

'Because he was jealous,' said Sandra. She said it quite deliberately. 'Jealous of David, there. Because I've been sleeping with him every night for weeks and I forgot to mention David's name. That's why.'

There was a strangled, awful, noise from David's armchair. She raised her head and looked at him. He was as white as a sheet. His mouth was open. He was gasping.

Sandra had a sudden, acute, awareness of what she had done. Not just then, by saying that, although that had cut him like a knife. But in the last few weeks. Looking at his face, she realised what she had done.

But she could not stay. She could not stay and face it. She could not face another scene tonight. She rose to her feet and stumbled. Because Ahmed stood up, and reached out a hand, and steadied her, she said to him, thickly: 'Please. Ahmed. Take me home, please, take me out of here.'

She started for the door, almost running. She said to David, over her shoulder, 'I'm sorry, Dave, I'm sorry.' He did not speak. He was staring at her, his face completely pale. Ahmed shrugged, avoided looking at him, got his coat. He closed the door quietly and followed Sandra to the street.

At first Sandra walked fast, almost ran, and Ahmed had to hurry to catch up with her. When he did he did not speak, or try to touch her, just kept up. After a few minutes she slowed down and they moved side by side, until her breathing was back to normal. He said at last: 'Where do you live, love? I'll take you there.'

Sandra shook her head.

'I can't go back,' she said. 'Not with my face like this. It's just not possible.'

He didn't ask her for alternatives. Although it was well after midnight, he appeared quite unworried to just walk round with her. After a bit, because David lived near the beach, it became apparent they were heading for the sea. The promenade was wide and deserted, the Channel black and glittering. They found an iron bench and sat down on it. It was a warm night, and the splashing of the waves on the shingle was peaceful and soothing.

'Christ, what a cow I am,' said Sandra, in the end. 'What a rotten little bitch.'

Ahmed said nothing.

'Poor David's face,' she said. 'I couldn't bear to stay and look at it. I couldn't bear to sit there and explain.'

She sighed.

'This must be quite a shock for you, all this,' she said. 'It's the first time I've met you since school, really. Except for that day. And all this happens. You're very calm about it.'

'Yeah,' said Ahmed. 'What else do you want? Have you got a better idea?'

'I don't expect you to believe this, Ahmed,' Sandra said. 'But I didn't even realise. I mean, I knew I'd hurt him when I said it, I intended it to hurt. But I never dreamed. We've been going out for ages, years, I bet he never mentioned *that* to you lot! I really thought it was all over. That he really didn't care.'

'You were provoked, you know,' said Ahmed. 'And that's to put it mildly. A story! Stroll on!'

Sandra gave a half laugh.

'Yeah,' she said. 'You've got a point, I spose. But I needn't have done it like I did.'

'No point in worrying, love,' said Ahmed. 'It's done. What can't be cured has to be endured, they say. He sort of asked for it.'

'Mm,' said Sandra.

They sat there, looking at the sea and stars for several minutes, in silence. Then Sandra said: 'Ahmed, what do you *think* of David? Really. I mean . . . about his attitude.'

To her surprise, Ahmed picked up her drift immediately.

'I know what you're on about,' he said. 'You mean why's

117

he so involved? Why's he mixed up in the Noor affair? What does he think of blacks?'

She nodded. He thought.

'I think it was a romantic thing at first,' he said. 'I think he fancied the idea of getting friends with the nignogs. I think Riccard Crawford was the one. He wanted to be approved of by the big black firebrand. Stupid really. The man's a prat.'

'Who? Riccard or David?'

'Riccard, I meant, but I'm being stupid. He's not a prat at all. But his political views get up my nose sometimes, that's all. They tend to put people's backs up, same as Kenny Baby's. People who should be on our side. The papers always rub it in. Whatever good the REC are doing they say they're making trouble and should let things take their course. Jeez! We'd all be dead with fascists if they did!'

'And David?' said Sandra. 'He's *on* the papers.'

'He's all right,' said Ahmed. 'At first I didn't like him. It was spooky, he was sort of sucking up to us. He used to treat you like an object in public – "look at me", like, "I'm friends with an Asian". But you grow out of it. It's a common thing.'

He laughed.

'You'd be surprised how common,' he said. 'But no, David's all right. He's one of the good guys. He's on the side of the angels.'

After a while, Ahmed looked at his watch.

'Look,' he said. 'What are you going to do? It's getting awful late. Why don't you come back to my place?'

Sandra was startled.

'It's quite legit,' he said. 'It's not a chat-up line, my Mum and Dad are there. And my sisters. We've got a spare room, that's all. You're welcome to sleep in it.'

Sandra was fazed. Being invited to an Asian's house was outside her experience. Ahmed picked up the thought.

'We're not from Outer Space, you know,' he said genially. 'We do have beds and that. We're quite like human beings in many ways!'

She shook her head.

118

'Sorry,' she said. 'I'm a fool. Just habit. Thank you, Ahmed, honestly, but I won't. There's no point in messing, I'll have to go home in the end. And they might be worried, anyway. I didn't say I'd be out late. I'll go back home.'

'I'll walk you,' he said.

'You won't,' she said. 'I can look after myself.'

He grinned.

'Looks like it,' he said. 'You're black and blue!'

Two minutes later, they had gone their separate ways. Funny, thought Sandra, as she walked along. All those years I knew him and I never knew. He seems a really nice guy. . .

SIXTEEN

Next morning, Sandra broke her golden rule. She stayed off work.

She awoke at the normal time, despite the stresses of the night before and the fact that it was very late before she got to bed. She lay between the sheets feeling terrible. She ached in her body, and her face was stiff and smarting. Her throat was sore.

In the bedroom next to hers, she heard her father bring her mother in a cup of tea. She panicked, because a minute later he would be in her room. She felt her enormous lip and her swollen cheek. She wondered how she could hide. Then she lay there.

When he opened the door, Sandra spoke in the dimness, before he had time to draw the curtains.

'I'm a bit battered, Dad, my face. Don't worry about it, and keep your voice down.'

Her father drew the curtains and came to the bed. He put her tea down on the bedside table and looked at her.

'Well,' he said. 'That's a right old mess, gal. Where were you last night, we were worried. Were you in a fight?'

Sandra got up onto one elbow and reached for her tea.

'Yes,' she said. 'Nothing serious, Dad. Nothing to get hung about. It's being in the police. It has this effect on people.'

She tried to smile, and winced.

'Oh,' she said. 'It hurts.'

Her father sat down on the bed with a creak of springs.

'But you weren't in uniform last night,' he said. 'You were in civvies. You were wearing that jacket over there.'

Sandra followed his eyes. She noticed, for the first time, that the jacket's collar was hanging off. There was a bloodstain on the blouse, draped over it.

'Yes,' she said. 'I got in a fight. It doesn't always matter if you're in uniform.'

He looked deeply depressed.

'God, gal,' he said. 'I don't want you beaten up like this. I don't want this sort of thing to happen.'

'No,' she said. 'It didn't do a lot for me, love. But it's not the end of the world. Only the wreck of the Hesperus, more like. Go and warn Mum, will you? Tell her it's nothing but a few cuts and bruises. She'll worry herself sick.'

She could have got away, at headquarters, she guessed, with blaming it on the march. There'd been so many injuries, and so much raw excitement, that she doubted if anyone would remember that she'd hardly got a scratch. But she could not be bothered. She got her mother – when she'd recovered from the shock – to ring up Union Street and say she wasn't well, just that. She didn't even worry about dreaming up an illness.

Mum tried to talk to her about it over coffee later in the morning, when Dad had gone to work. But Sandra made it clear she didn't want to know. It had been a routine thing, she said, a brawl. She just wanted to rest and get over it, it wasn't worth the candle of talking out. Her mother didn't believe her, otherwise why the telephoned excuse? But her mother was learning fast about Sandra, and police work, and things like that. She did not push her luck.

Sandra reintroduced the telephone routine she'd used on David. She told her mother to do the answering, and just to say she wasn't in. There were three calls in the morning from a man her mother did not recognise – Brian, obviously. But there were none from David. Sandra, thinking about the night before, imagined that this time the cure would have been complete. She missed him quite badly, on and off, and was tempted from time to time to ring him up. She wondered if he had gone to work or if he would have been too upset. That felt conceited, but she remembered his

121

shocked white face with a pang of pain and guilt. What a bitch she'd been. Not least for the way she'd used it as a weapon. She might have known he loved her, or at least had something left. She tried to imagine how she would have felt if he'd revealed he'd been sleeping with someone else. But she could not. But what a bitch. She wondered if he'd ever speak to her again.

After lunch, her mother hobbled the few hundred yards to the shops to get some nice things for tea – soft things that Sandra would appreciate, like strawberries and a chocolate layer cake. She also brought back the early edition of the *Echo*. Sandra, sitting in an armchair sipping a cup of tea cool enough not to hurt her lip, read it with interest.

The march had made the front page, of course, as the main story. The headline said: 'Gangs of thugs break up Allahi demo' and it was a factual account of how the police lines had been broken and a pitched battle taken place. There were quotes from senior policemen saying the whole thing had been regrettable, but their men had been overwhelmed. Another quote, from a leading local councillor, criticised the marchers, and suggested that their action had been provocative, and they had hampered the police – many of whom had been injured – in their duty. The fact that there had been seventeen arrests – all but three of them marchers – was reported, but not remarked upon.

Lower down the page, and decorated with five pictures of whites and Asians with bandages and bloody faces, was an eye-witness report by David Tanner. It described how he had seen policemen 'helping' thugs and kicking and punching marchers indiscriminately. It said that as a reporter he considered the police had done as little as they possibly could to aid the column when it came under attack, and in many instances appeared to condone it, if not actively participate. There were quotes from several other people, including Kenny Baby Shaw who called for a full inquiry, and Asians including Ahmed Rashid who complained of specific beatings by police. An *Echo* photographer, Phillip Dyson, described how his camera had been snatched from him as he tried to film two policemen roughing up a black, and jumped on in the gutter. At the end of the story was a quote from a senior police officer. It said that no complaints had been received about the conduct of policemen from any quarter, but if there were any, they would be dealt with according to the normal procedure. As there had been none, however, it was impossible for the police to comment on vague allegations of misconduct.

Finally, there was a short leader, headed 'March of Shame'. It suggested that reports of police irregularity were never to be taken at face value, as they were usually politically motivated. However, the allegations of police misconduct at this event were so widespread and vociferous that they either had some foundation in fact – however slight – or were the product of a 'carefully orchestrated' campaign of propaganda. It was necessary, said the leader, that the facts should be ascertained by the proper authorities 'as a matter of urgency'. Lastly, though, it had to be said that the marchers themselves must bear a heavy burden of responsibility. It was inevitable that if people banded together in this way to make a protest that was essentially political, it would provoke a reaction, however unreasonable. The police, as ever, found themselves in the middle. Everyone was against them, and they had to be fair to everyone. Whatever they did, however hard they tried, however impartial they were – everyone would claim otherwise. It was an iniquitous burden on a fine body of men and women doing an impossible job extremely well.

Sandra read it several times, with fascination. It was only when she turned at last to the back page, to the rest of the day's main news, that she noticed the Stop Press. The Home Office had announced the date on which Noor Allahi – alias Mohammed Mansoor – was to be deported. All in all she thought, the police had won hands down. Despite David's story, they could hardly complain that the *Echo*'s coverage was biased, and they'd got what they wanted. The naming of deportation day was a very pretty touch indeed.

About an hour later the phone rang once more, and Sandra decided she might as well answer it. It was Brian, and his attitude appalled her. He was as near as dammit unrepentant about the night before, and he appeared more interested in slagging off the *Echo*, and all journalists. Sandra had been wrong. The very fact there'd been a hint of criticism had been enough. Police opinion of the local rag had reached an all-time low.

She began to get the drift behind the drift as the call went on. Brian was mounting a personal attack on David. What a slimy little no-hoper he was, what a leftie, what a pervert. At last he asked her what was wrong with her, and why she was not at work.

Sandra realised, by now, that he was not joking. But her mind was boggling, just the same. She was in no mood for messing about, though.

'Brian,' she said. 'I think you must be mad. You may not remember this, but you tried to strangle me last night. You–'

He guffawed.

'Rubbish, girl,' he said. 'I wouldn't harm a fly! And anyway, I apologised. I'll say it again. I'm sorry if I hurt you, honestly. But you had it coming, you must admit. You must admit you asked for it.'

Sandra looked at the telephone in amazement. She was speechless.

'Anyway,' said Brian. 'That's all water under the bridge. Can I see you tonight, to talk? Where can I pick you up?'

'Brian,' she said. 'I'm trying to keep my cool, so listen hard and keep your mouth shut. You'll never know how close I got to reporting you last night, you'll never know. I could have had you done for grievous bodily harm, assault and battery, and . . . and attempted rape if I wanted to rub it in. And if you say a word I will. I promise you, Mister, I bloody will.'

She could hear him breathing at the other end. She heard him swallow.

'I know what you're thinking,' she said. 'You're thinking it's your word against mine. Well it's not. After I left your

124

place, I went to David Tanner's. He had friends in, and one of them had a camera. I told them all about it, and they took a lot of photographs. If you make trouble, Brian, I'll drop you in it. I'll drop you so far in it they wouldn't even let you make the tea. Not in HQ. Not anywhere. Except for prison if you're lucky. D'you get it?'

At the end of the line, she heard another swallow. She went on.

'I also stayed the night at David's, and I slept with him,' she said. 'I told him lots of things, Brian, and I mentioned you by name. I told him plenty, all about us, every last damn detail. And he's Press. Lay off me, Brian, just leave me quite alone. If you start anything – *anything* – there'll be hell to pay. If I hear just one rumour, just one nasty tale. Bingo. That's it. You're in it. I told him everything.'

She put the phone down, and leaned against the wall. Then she walked through the kitchen to the garden, where her mother was sitting in the sun.

'It was for me,' she said. 'A bit of business. Would you like a cup of tea?'

A few days later, when the telephone rang and Sandra answered it, it was Ahmed. She was surprised, and her voice must have shown it.

'I was ringing for David, in a way,' he said, half apologetically. 'Well, instead of him, actually. There's something he says you ought to see, but he . . . but he . . . well, he doesn't want to see you, actually.'

Sandra made a neutral noise. That made her feel quite bad.

'Can you come out?' asked Ahmed. 'How's your face? Are you fit to be seen in public?'

'Oh yeah,' said Sandra. 'It's almost back to normal. Large as life and twice as ugly!'

'Well, will you come?' he said. 'I could meet you in the White Swan if you like. You know, near the common. That's about halfway for both of us.'

'Yes,' she said. 'All right. Yes, I'll see you there, then.'

When she reached the pub, Ahmed was already there. He waved from a booth then went to the bar and got her a gin and tonic. There was a big brown envelope on the table, and he pushed it to one side when he sat opposite. He was drinking pale ale.

'Cheers,' he said. 'You're right about your face. It's looking fine.'

'Yeah,' said Sandra. 'I've been skiving off of work because of it. I'll have to go back now, there's nothing for it.'

'What will that mean?' asked Ahmed. 'Will they put you back on the so-called murder hunt? Or have they dropped that yet?'

'You never know till you get there,' said Sandra. 'You do what they tell you. I'm only a cadet, a sort of dogsbody. I don't really do a lot. Just hang around and rubberneck. I don't know about the murder.'

Ahmed took a mouthful from his glass. His eye was still puffed up, the skin beneath it badly split.

'It'll be a blessing when they do drop the pretence,' he said. 'If they'd just let it die away and stop cracking on they were looking for the murderer. It's causing a hell of a lot of bad feeling at Hindley.'

'Mm,' said Sandra, non-committally. 'It was pretty awful when I was down there. At the caravan. That was early days, first time.'

'It's much worse now,' said Ahmed. 'The Special Branch are in and they harass people like mad. They're always doing passport checks and things like that. They're going door to door as well. They're bastards.'

Not so long ago Sandra would have argued, or been upset, or dubious, even angry. But now she was not surprised. It was only a small step from what she'd seen, even at the start.

'They're not looking for a murderer,' said Ahmed. 'They're looking for illegal immigrants. It's a disaster. I've never seen such fear and hatred.'

'Is Noor illegal?' Sandra said.

'What?' he said. 'How do you mean? Of course he's not! You know that!'

'Oh don't get angry, Ahmed,' said Sandra. 'I don't mean to sound as if I don't believe. It's just the name thing, I suppose. It's years since Rehana Rasool first told me, I've forgotten. And anyway –' she flashed him a smile – 'I don't suppose you'd try and save him any the less if he was illegal, would you?'

Ahmed looked at her soberly, then slowly smiled.

'No,' he said. 'I suppose you're right. Fancy you remembering Rehana. She's back in India now. She was in your class, wasn't she? Anyway – the name. There's nothing unusual about it, it's just you English and your obsession with formality. I don't know the exact reason, but it could be something like this. Say Mr Mansoor and his wife had tried – and failed – to have a baby. He was quite old, you know, Noor's *chacha*, much older than his wife. Let's say they pray to Allah for a child, and promise that if he blesses them they will not use the family name. Perhaps it has been cursed, or jinxed, you know these village people with their superstitious nonsenses. So when a son is born – they keep their promise. They call him Noor Allahi, light from God, you know? For a whole sub-Continent, no trouble. Perfectly logical. And then he comes to England, poor little sod.'

'But why does he call himself Mansoor, then? He did at school, a lot. We've got him down on the family tree as both. It's so haphazard.'

Ahmed was preoccupied.

'Light from God,' he said. 'Poor little Noor. It's no wonder no one's religious much these days. If every light from God was as weak and feeble as him . . .' He finished his beer. 'Why ask?' he said. 'You know the English. A name is important. A fixed thing. "I'm Noor Allahi but my *chacha's* name is Mansoor" – Pah. Easier for him to call himself Mohammed Mansoor. It's a good enough name. Anything would do, except for you lot. Want another drink?'

'I'll get them,' said Sandra, standing up.

'And there's another thing,' said Ahmed. 'I've just called

Yusuf Mansoor his *chacha*. That would set the cat among the pigeons at the police station. It means uncle. I call my dad *chacha* too, it's a normal thing. And I was born in England, I've got a British passport. I call the milkman *chacha* too. He's a Bangladeshi.'

When Sandra returned, Ahmed had pulled a sheaf of papers from the envelope and was leafing through them. They were photocopies of rather badly typed pages. He pushed them back inside and thanked her for the drink. He swallowed and smacked his lips.

'I brought you this to read,' he said. 'It's a letter from Noor Allahi. He wrote it out by hand and the solicitor smuggled it out of Bentham. We had it typed. Well, KB did it, and his wife. Sara.'

'Why do you want me to read it, though?'

Ahmed smiled, wryly.

'I wouldn't be surprised,' he said, 'if it wasn't an attempt by David to keep in contact. But he wouldn't come himself, when it got down to it. I think he hopes you'll get in touch.'

Sandra licked her lips.

'Yeah,' she said. 'How is he? Is he all right?'

'Bearing up,' said Ahmed. 'We're all feeling the strain a bit because of the Noor affair. He's been taken off the story by the newseditor guy. He's not allowed to touch it. They found out he was connected with the REC. There were ructions. So our coverage is down. Not that there's a lot that we can do.'

'Are you going to appeal? Against the order?'

Ahmed did not smile.

'No appeal,' he said. 'This is Britain. Under the 1971 Immigration Act all such matters are entirely in the hands of the Home Office. No reasons given, no questions answered, no appeals allowed.'

'Oh,' said Sandra. 'Oh.'

'We've got the local MP on our side at last, despite the fact he's a diehard Tory,' Ahmed went on. 'That's something. But all he can do is make the noises, like the rest of us. We're just hoping the noise gets loud enough. So far the national

128

Press and television have done nothing. They call themselves a service.'

'Oh,' said Sandra, again. She drank some gin. 'Can I take them home, the papers?'

'Oh yes,' said Ahmed. 'But don't show them to anyone, of course. If Riccard knew, he'd tear our heads off, mine and David's. But David trusts you. So do I.'

'In spite of everything,' she said. 'Poor David.'

'While there's life there's hope,' said Ahmed. 'I told the silly sod to come himself, or even with me. But he wouldn't. There you go.'

'Yeah,' said Sandra. 'I'll read it, Ahmed, and I'll get in . . . And I'll. Well. Yeah. There you go . . .'

SEVENTEEN

By chance, about a week after she'd gone back to work, Sandra was given the opportunity to go to Bentham, where Allahi had been held since shortly after his confession. She jumped at it, and not just because it would get her out of the station for a while. For ever since she had read his long, rambling and often confused letter, she had been uncomfortable, depressed and unsure. She had been aware of a growing feeling, an idea that she did not want to accept, which had been blossoming in her mind. It was to do with resigning, leaving the force, getting out, and it was grinding her down. She felt, however foolishly, that a visit to the 'scene' might clear her brain.

It was not only the letter that had put her into this peculiar state. Moving around headquarters, assiduously avoiding any contact with Brian, had not helped. It had not been difficult, because he had specific work to do, while she was sent here and there to help and learn and fetch the tea. But there was tension in the air between them, and it kept her constantly aware. She stuck as closely as possible to Terry, and without asking what was up he supported her. It was he who engineered the trip to the remand centre.

It was a dull, cool day, when even florid Terry was not sweating. They had about twenty miles to go and would probably be away for several hours. To Sandra, it felt a real relief. She relaxed rapidly in the car, and once they'd got clear of the city traffic, she found she could chat about the visit almost idly.

'What's Bentham like?' she asked. 'Is it horrible like that

famous one up North? Grisly Risley or whatever they call it?'

'As bad or worse,' said Terry. 'They all are. Another strand in the rich fabric of British injustice. The people in them are on remand, right? They're not convicted of anything, not "in prison". And you get all sorts. Kids, nuts, thugs, hardened criminals – all mixed in together. For months on end, sometimes. It's insane. There's been half a dozen suicides in Bentham, in the last few years. More maybe, I can't remember.'

'Christ,' said Sandra.

'Indeed,' said Terry. 'He'd have a fit if he returned to earth, poor sod. He'd go back up to Heaven like a shot. And if he had any decency he'd kick his father's arse all round the place for the monumental cock-up he made when he created it.'

Sandra hooted with laughter.

'God, you are a cynic, Terry! You ought to watch it, you know. You could get struck down dead!'

'A chance I'll have to take,' said Terry. 'I'm not a cynic though, far from it. Bentham is a bastard. A disgrace. It looks like a prison camp and that's more or less what it is. A concentration camp. Despicable.'

'I didn't know you were a socialist,' said Sandra.

He snorted.

'You don't half say funny things, Miss Patterson,' he said. 'What's all this stuff that Brian Updike's putting round?'

Sandra's stomach clenched. He'd caught her completely on the hop. She went bright red and stared into her lap.

'Oh,' she mumbled. 'I don't know. I didn't know he was.'

Terry drove in silence for a while, concentrating on overtaking someone. They were on a country road, and it was narrow.

'Well he's not exactly putting it round. He told me, but then he considers me a mate. I suggested it was the sort of thing he shouldn't spread too far.'

Sandra looked out of the window at the fields. Everything was dull in the fine drizzle that had settled in. She remembered her threat to Brian, on the phone. Fat lot of good that had done, apparently.

'What's he saying?' she said quietly. 'What sort of thing?'

'Well, all the usual stuff,' said Terry. 'He told me what a little slut you are, how you go for anything in trousers, all that muck. A few of the choicer refinements you adopt.'

Sandra looked curiously at Terry, from the corner of her eyes, to see if he was enjoying this. It seemed an extraordinary way of telling her. But his face was calm, composed. His eyes flicked into the mirror, his hands moved on the wheel.

'You're very frank,' she said at last. 'Are you expecting something? Is this your way of telling me that . . . that you and me should . . .'

He expelled air from his nostrils, sharply.

'No,' he said. 'I consider you my friend, is all. I remember what we went through once, together, in a boat. I told Brian Updike that if he said stuff like that to anybody else I'd cripple him. I think he got the message.'

'Oh,' she said. 'I'm sorry. Thanks. Thank you, Terry. Very much.'

'Don't make a meal of it, gal,' he said. '*De rien*, as the Frogs would say. Think nothing of it.'

After a minute or so, Sandra said: 'I did go out with him, you know. I did . . . sleep with him. My boyfriend didn't know.'

'We all make mistakes, love,' said Terry, humorously. 'I think if I slept with Updike I'd omit to mention it, as well. A definite lapse in your impeccable good taste.'

'God, what a swine,' said Sandra. 'He beat me up, he almost strangled me, the night of that march. That's why I stayed off work. I told him if he ever said a word to anyone I'd have him up for rape or something. What a swine.'

'He is a swine,' said Terry. 'But he's more a mess. He's *blessé de la guerre*. Walking wounded. You meet a lot of crippled people in the police. It's a lousy way to run a life. He's been married twice, as well. I bet you didn't know that, did you?'

She shook her head. She was surprised.

'He only ever mentions one,' said Terry. 'The one he hates. The one who's got the kids. His first wife ran off too, though. It's a hard life, in the force.'

Sandra said: 'He never seems to see the children. He mentioned it a lot.'

'Yeah,' said Terry. 'He used to beat her up. The wife. He hates her and despises her. He only got very limited access in the courts. It broke him up. I'd have warned you, but it didn't seem my place. I hope you didn't get too badly hurt.'

'Oh,' said Sandra. 'Did you know, then? That we were going out?'

'Most people did,' said Terry. 'There's not much that's a secret in that place. It's a hotbed.'

After they had been driving for a few more minutes, Terry drew into the car park of a small country pub.

'We're going to be irregular,' he said. 'I hope you don't mind breaking rules, but it's a way of life to a hardened cop like me. This pub's run by a mate of mine. He'll serve us round the back.'

As it was not yet lunchtime, the pub was deserted. They went round the garden to the rear door, and were soon sitting in a tiny old room. The landlord brought Terry a pint and Sandra a gin, then went back to the kitchen after a brief chat. Sandra stretched her legs out and relaxed.

'This is the life,' she said. 'It's a pity we can't just stay all day. Get quietly plastered and have a meal.'

'Yes,' said Terry. 'And of all the places we've to go, it's Bentham.'

'Will we see Allahi?' asked Sandra, suddenly. 'You know, the little Asian lad that the Special Branch took away?'

'I know who Noor Allahi is,' said Terry. 'Don't remind me. No. We won't see anyone. I've just got to deliver some papers, that's all. Collect some forms and statements. You probably needn't even come inside. It's a depressing place.'

Sandra spun her drink round in her glass.

'Terry,' she said shyly. 'Can I ask you something serious? About Allahi? Do you reckon he was mistreated over this? Do you reckon they forced him to confess?'

Terry sighed.

'I wouldn't know for sure,' he said. 'I wasn't in on it, was I, I'm in uniform. Why do you ask?'

'Well,' said Sandra. 'Well, there was that stuff in the canteen that time. You and Brian and Dennis. And the Special Branch were mentioned. And . . . and . . .'

She stopped. She wondered if she should mention the Noor Allahi letter. She'd thought about it almost constantly for days, but she still could not come to terms with it. It was a horrifying document, although it only seemed to confirm what she'd suspected. Since his arrest, and particularly since the Special Branch had taken over, Noor Allahi – if he was to be believed – had been treated with appalling viciousness. She decided not to mention it, even to Terry. She had promised she would not.

'And what?' he said. 'Well, never mind, what's the point in beating about the bush? Yes, love, if you want it straight, I wouldn't be at all surprised. Whether or not the confession's genuine I couldn't say, I wouldn't have the foggiest. But as to if it was kicked out of him or not. Yeah. I think it's highly likely. That's being straight. All right?'

Sandra's stomach hollowed. Somehow it would have been better if Terry had denied it, said it was unlikely. She would have believed him, and she would have been totally reassured. She needed to be reassured, desperately. She looked at the table top.

'In a way,' he went on, 'it's a game, all this. Everything, this whole shooting match of crime and punishment and heroes and villians, it's only a game. There are rules, and when you've been playing long enough, you get to know them. The trouble is, it can get very one-sided, if you follow me. I mean – half the players don't know they're playing. In little Noor Allahi's case, I guess, he didn't even know he'd been invited.'

Sandra glanced at him to see if he was smiling. He was not. She presumed he had been trying to make her feel better, though. Odd way of doing it.

'The race thing's brought in a whole new section, see,'

Terry said. 'It's not totally fixed yet. The grandmasters at the top have only decided on the guidelines. Against Allahi, the moves aren't fixed.'

Sandra still felt flat.

'You're not a racist,' she said. 'Why are so many, in the force? The whole thing reeks of racism.'

Terry half-smiled, ruefully.

'I'm not a racist, aren't I?' he said. 'What is a racist, anyway? How would you define it? What about that black man, Riccard Crawford? He doesn't like whites, that's for sure. Or Tony Gardiner. He'd have said he was, we used to argue about it. And look what happened to him.'

Sandra was silent. Terry had never spoken about Tony since his death. He took a pull from his pint pot, and wiped the foam from his lips.

'Well, all right,' he said. 'I do know racist coppers. Lots of them. But I know a lot more desperate ones. We're the PBI, love, the Poor Bloody Infantry. We're racist 'cause we're meant to be. If you want to know why the Special Branch smacked up Noor Allahi, work it backwards to his "crime". It's the grandmasters who decide on that, the politicians. We're not to blame.'

Sandra was disappointed, and it showed. She hadn't expected to hear Terry making what sounded like excuses. He threw back his head and laughed.

'Don't look so down, gal,' he said. 'It's not as simple as it looks. The police force in this country's in a mess, it's chaos in some places, you know that. Of course we're to blame in one way, but there's more to it. There's things going on today in good old, smug old, England that wouldn't have been out of place in Hitler's Germany, and they don't just come from us. We're the soldiers, we're victims, too. Some of us obey bad orders 'cause we've got to, and some of us have grown to like bad orders. But we didn't make them. We didn't start the war.'

He took another drink, and looked at his watch.

'And now we've got to go,' he said. 'That's an order – which I require you to obey! When we get to Bentham, if it's

135

not raining too hard, wind your window down and listen. Sometimes, if the wind's right, and the inmates are unhappy enough, you can hear them screaming. It's horrible, diabolical, and you can't blame it on the police. Who can you blame it on though, Sandra? You'll have to think about it, love. I can't help you.'

It was raining hard when they got outside, and they did not talk for the last few miles to Bentham. Sandra waited in the car as Terry had suggested, and looked at the long low lines of huts behind the barbed wire. She opened up her window for a while, but heard nothing save the heavy, beating rain.

She thought of many things, but her mind was no longer wandering. She remembered passages from Allahi's letter clearly, passages that she'd hardly believed when she'd read them, until she'd talked to Terry. She remembered that his solicitor – in Allahi's words – had described the Special Branch as 'secret police, allowed to hurt you and carry guns.' She remembered how he'd appealed to the police doctors to help him in the cells, to tell people what was happening, and had been ignored.

It was a game, Terry had said, only a game. He hadn't meant that as an absolute, she knew it, and he'd told her plainly just who made the 'rules'. She wasn't sure if she believed him totally, and she knew she would have to think it all through, worry out the problems. But while he was inside the remand centre, she made her big decision. She was going to leave the police.

If it was a game, she wasn't going to play. She'd had enough.

EIGHTEEN

Although it was hard to do, Sandra did not mention her decision to Terry on the way back to town. He started talking about his impending holiday in France with his wife and kids, 'to get the taste of Bentham' out of his mouth. Sandra got into the swing of it, and asked him a question, mockingly.

'How come you're so happy and level-headed, with a happy marriage and all that stuff?' she said. 'When all the other coppers in the world are falling into bits?'

He grinned.

'I'm a superman,' he said. 'And I listen to reggae music while drinking beer and making love!'

But as they drove into the Union Street car park and pulled to a halt in the rain, Sandra said her piece. It was only fair. He looked at her in silence for a while. The rain drummed on the roof.

'I wish you wouldn't, gal,' he said. 'The police force needs you. And that's not joking, either. Don't make a snap decision, love.'

Sandra reddened. She said, awkwardly: 'No . . . Well, I . . . Well, haven't *you* ever thought of getting out? You're too nice really, Terry.'

'That's balls,' he said. 'We need all the nice ones we can get. But yes, I've considered it. And no, I wouldn't go. I'm staying.'

'Why, though?'

'As an antidote?' he said, half smiling. 'To shits like Brian Updike? No, seriously though. I'm staying because I'm needed In the deep end. I told you earlier what I thought of

137

politicians. They won't help. The rot comes from the top. This country's desperate, and the bastards will not help. I'm the knight in shining armour. The Lone Ranger.'

He stopped, and dragged his hand across his face, looking desperately discouraged.

'I'm nothing, and there's not a lot I can do,' he said. 'But I'm staying on. Don't leave us, Sandra. I'm deadly serious.'

He opened his door abruptly and got out into the pouring rain. They ran into the station.

That evening, Sandra thought a lot of the things they'd talked about, but her mind was jumbled, jumpy, in a whirl. She had a bath, and pondered for ages what she ought to wear. She had agreed to go and have a meal with David. Ostensibly to take Noor's letter back. And talk.

To her astonishment, when he'd made the date, David had said he would cook. She bought a bottle of wine at the supermarket and rang the doorbell, formally. When he answered it they both coloured. He tried to kiss her on the lips, but the bottle got in the way. He stammered: 'Why didn't you use your key?' And she joked tactlessly: 'In case you were in bed with somebody.' It was all rather awkward.

Inevitably, the dinner was a Chinese takeaway, that he'd put to keep warm in a too-hot oven. The crispy noodles were crisp all right – downright inedible. But they persevered, largely in silence, out of sheer embarrassment. They shot Sandra's wine down fast though, and another bottle that David had bought. After half a litre each, things began to free up a little.

'Have you read it yet?' he asked. 'The Noor Allahi thing? What did you think?'

Sandra chewed on, at a piece of oven-toughened beef. She wondered what she ought to say.

'That's not a very easy question to ask a copper, David,' she said at last, but mildly. 'You make me feel like pig in the middle.'

'Very good,' he said. 'That's the first time I've ever heard

138

you use that word about the force, Sandra. But you're not really bad enough to be a pig. A little piggy maybe. Piggy in the middle.'

Sandra decided to laugh. The ice was breaking after all.

'I thought it was awful, actually. To tell the truth, it made me quite ashamed.'

David nodded, seriously.

'It's pretty diabolical,' he said. 'I shouldn't have suggested showing you, I suppose. But I wanted to get in touch. And . . . And. Well, to be quite ridiculously honest, I suppose I wanted to get at you. I wanted to have a dig. I wanted to hurt you, if I could.'

'Yes,' said Sandra. 'I can't say I'm surprised. I treated you like a fink. I'm sorry.'

David was chewing. She went on.

'Anyway, it had the desired effect. It opened my eyes a bit. It made me see that you and Shaw and Rastus and that lot weren't just a gang of nutters and nasty revolutionaries like everyone says you are.' She took a drop of wine. 'No, even that's not quite true,' she said. 'I think I'd already decided. But seeing it in black and white. Well.'

He said, very cautiously: 'Do you still . . . Are you and that policeman still –'

'Good God no,' said Sandra. 'Nobody beats me up more than once. Nobody beats me up at all, and gets away with it.'

'Yes,' he said. 'You're a hard lady.'

Sandra almost told the truth. That she hadn't really liked Brian anyway, that she didn't really know how it had all happened, what had been going on. But she didn't. It was early days yet. She wasn't *that* sure what was going on here, between her and David. She merely gave a little smirk, and told him in a cod American accent: 'Better not forget it, baby. You could get into trouble.'

Later on they went for a walk on the seafront. The rain had cleared but it was very fresh and windy. They steered away from all but simple topics, and after a while David put his arm around her waist. When they got back to the flat he asked her, with a tremble in his voice: 'Are we going to . . .?'

She had already decided, walking by the sea, while they had talked inanities. She went to the lavatory, then joined him in the bedroom. But it wasn't very good. David was nervous, and awkward, and infuriatingly apologetic, reminding her of a fawning, pathetic sort of dog, desperate to be loved. Afterwards he tried to cry, and questioned her endlessly about Brian and why she had done it. She tried to be kind, but she was impatient. It seemed to her that everything was over now. There was nothing left.

Two days after sending in her letter of resignation, Sandra was called in to see Inspector Thompson. Although he was nominally in overall charge of trainees, she had never actually spoken to him, and she was rather frightened. In fact, it had come as a shock to be asked to explain herself at all. She had thought long and hard before putting pen to paper – mainly because of Terry's response – but once she'd decided, and got it written down, and stuck it in the post, she'd somehow seen the whole thing as being over. She would work out a few weeks notice, then she would leave, just like that. And that would be an end to the whole caboodle; the entire can of worms could be forgotten.

Sandra had told no one of what was in her head since her talk with Terry, and she had merely smiled jerkily when he himself had asked if she had changed her mind. Her letter had been brief and functional, giving no reasons at all. Standing outside Thompson's office, she was fluttery and nervous. She was completely unprepared.

When the green light outside the office flashed to 'enter', Sandra did so. The room was quite large, and very quiet. She could see the harbour through the picture window, but she could hear nothing. It must be double glazed. Inspector Thompson, a smallish, rather soft-looking man with a paunch, indicated a seat to her. He was sitting behind a desk, that was empty except for an Anglepoise lamp and a blotter. On the blotter her letter lay, white and forlorn.

'Cadet Patterson,' said the inspector, when she had sat

down. 'This has come as a great shock to us here. Everybody thinks of you as an absolutely excellent potential police-person. Is this your last thought on the subject, or are you open to persuasion?'

His voice, surprisingly, was quite warm and friendly. Sandra, who had been expecting a tougher approach, was thrown.

'I'm afraid, sir,' she began. Her voice squeaked, and she cleared her throat. He smiled encouragement.

'Take your time, Miss Patterson,' he said. 'There is absolutely no need to hurry.'

'Thank you, sir,' she said. 'But I'm afraid . . . well, that *is* my last word. It hasn't been an easy decision, I assure you. Ever since I was a child I wanted to be in the police. I'm afraid it didn't work out, that's all. I've got to go.'

He looked down at the letter and tapped it with his fingernail.

'It doesn't give a lot away,' he said. 'Are you prepared to do me the courtesy of elucidating your reasons?'

Despite the friendliness, Sandra was still jumpy. Her mouth dried.

'I don't wish to be discourteous,' she said. 'But I think perhaps I'd better. . . . Well.'

He looked levelly at her.

'I understand it has something to do with the Mohammed Mansoor case,' he said. He watched her reaction. 'I see that you are surprised by that. Well don't be, Miss Patterson. We have to keep a friendly eye open on our younger members, you realise. A fatherly eye, I might say.'

She nodded, dumb.

'I imagine you have seen the document,' he said. He smiled. 'The gospel according to Mohammed Mansoor. Or Noor Allahi, to use his proper name. You are young, Sandra, if you do not mind me saying so. Did it not occur to you that this young man might be lying?'

Sandra was amazed. Not only that he had guessed she'd seen the document, but that he knew of its existence. She wondered how, exactly.

'Assuming that you have read it,' he went on, 'I *will* say that I cannot fault you on compassion. And I will add to *that*, that compassion is a quality we cannot have enough of in the force. But I fear I must disabuse you. That document, unfortunately, is a farrago of lies. Better men than you, Miss Patterson – more experienced men and women than you – have come to the conclusion that Noor Allahi is certainly an illegal immigrant and possibly a parricide.'

Sandra shivered involuntarily. It had not occurred to her that there was still any question that Allahi might have killed his father. Inspector Thompson paused.

'I see the term disturbs you,' he went on. 'But I use it advisedly, Miss Patterson. Do not let your compassion and inexperience run away with you yet again. Noor Allahi has not been charged with murdering his father, and he quite possibly never will be. But that, sadly, is no guarantee that he was not responsible for that truly dreadful crime.'

He leaned forward suddenly, and peered at her across the desk.

'And do not forget that, young lady,' he told her. 'Do not forget just what a dreadful crime it was. Do not forget the victim, either. That is an unfortunate tendency among certain. . . . Well, never mind. Suffice it to say that you are not the sole licensee of compassion in this force. It is arrogant to presume that you are.'

'I don't,' she said. Her voice was almost a whisper. She could not look across the desk, but she had an image of the man regarding her. There was a half-smile on his face, he was explaining her stupidity away, he was trying to put her right. She could hardly believe it was happening.

Inspector Thompson placed his elbows on his desk and his finger-tips together. He pursed his lips.

'All around you, Miss Patterson,' he said, 'people are afraid. Afraid of what is happening to our society. Afraid of the breakdown that is apparent in the rule of law, in what is commonly known as law and order. Afraid of the rending of the country's social fabric. People think that crime must be combated, that the criminal mind is ruthless, unremitting, and becoming all-pervasive. That it must be fought, equally ruthlessly, with every possible weapon. Do you think them wrong? Do you not agree? Do you think we should not fight?'

She had to say something. She swallowed, and decided to be bold.

'Of course I do,' she said. 'That's why I joined the police. But I'm afraid. . . . Some of the things. . . . The Noor Allahi thing . . .'

She tailed off. When it came to it, she didn't have the guts. Inspector Thompson did not bat an eyelid.

'I have told you,' he said, 'that the Allahi document is nonsense. More important, in my view, is your response to it. For it seems to me that you are suggesting something very nasty. Even by this simple letter of resignation, you are suggesting that there has been serious misconduct in this very building. You may not realise it entirely – I shall take the charitable view – but by your apparent acceptance of that document, you are accusing your fellow officers of insensitivity, illegality, and misconduct bordering on the brutal. Well?'

Sandra licked her lips. She was feeling panicky inside, seriously confused. There was so little doubt in the inspector, he was so completely confident. He talked of 'misconduct bordering on the brutal' with an almost jolly air. Bordering! Hell. He was either crazy or a liar, he must be. But he didn't seem to be. He seemed calm, rational – and above all, honest. She had a swoop of terror in her stomach. Maybe he was right. And she was wrong. Maybe Noor Allahi –

'I believe the document,' she blurted out. 'And other officers in this –'

'Stop!' he said. 'Do not presume to –'

Sandra stopped, and so did Thompson. His face was flushed with anger. Sandra was thirsty, desperate for something to wet her mouth. She had not wanted this, had not intended to talk about her reasons. Inspector Thompson calmed rapidly.

'I apologise,' he said. 'I must always bear in mind your

age. It is entirely clear to me that you are misguided, not malicious. But really, Sandra. You must try to learn. You must try to understand the other point of view. Now listen.'

He smiled winningly, and Sandra smiled sadly back. She could see no alternative.

'Look, my dear,' he said. 'I'm not going to pretend to you that there are not areas of regret. In all police work things occur that should not, in an ideal world. But the world is not ideal, now is it? And sometimes, corners do get cut, I won't deny it.'

He smiled again, as if expecting her to speak. Sandra had nothing to say.

'But cutting corners to achieve a necessary end is a far, far different thing from what you apparently think could happen in this force,' he said. 'And that is what I'm trying to fathom in you. I find it frankly impossible, you see, to understand that you would rather credit the scurrilous allegations of politically motivated people than your own colleagues. And I find it extraordinary that you should be prepared to resign – to give up a promising career – over one case which you do not fully comprehend.'

Inspector Thompson moved his head quizzically, but Sandra remained silent. She felt the breakdown was complete. They were talking of two different worlds. They were on different planets.

'Sandra,' he said. 'I will be frank. Any organisation may have rotten apples, even the police. Now I happen to know for a fact that the officers in this force are neither brutal, nor partial, nor dishonest. But if you have any evidence to the contrary – however flimsy – you have only to bring it forward, and it will be thoroughly investigated. Make your complaint, and it will be dealt with. I give you my word.'

This time, Sandra guessed, she was probably not expected to reply. She still believed him honest, she was convinced of it. Somehow, she found the knowledge devastating. She felt shattered by it. She stared at her hands. They were gripped together in her lap. After a reasonable pause, Inspector

Thompson continued. His voice was warm, and strong.

'There's the rub, you see,' he said. 'We do need evidence, and we so rarely get it. Allegations, yes, they are two a penny. But we need facts. Anyone can throw mud, and sadly, much of it so often sticks. You are young, Sandra, but you are surely not so young that you cannot understand this simple proposition: support the rule of law, support evidence, support the police. Or we return inevitably to the swamp. It is a question of morals, you see, morals and morality. Let the race relations industry make their sly attacks on behalf of this young criminal. Let the media add their pennyweight of distortion. But let you and I and all of us uphold morality and the rule of law.'

There was silence. Sandra raised her head to look at him. His face was earnest, grave, with just the hint of an encouraging smile at the corners of his lips. Sandra surprised herself.

'I can't stand much more of this,' she said. She started quietly, but her voice got rapidly stronger. 'I can't see why it's wrong to say so when a policeman breaks the law. I can't see why anyone who criticises is throwing mud. People wouldn't make the allegations if they didn't need to, it's because we're bad they hate us. They want us cleaning up and they want it soon. They want someone to realise that we've got to be stopped from going barmy for our *own* good as well as everyone else's. It's you who's got to see, not me! It's people like *you* who are immoral!'

Inspector Thompson stood up. She'd cracked his composure.

'Miss Patterson –'

'No listen,' she said. She stood up, too. Her voice was high, she was almost shouting. 'No listen. It's not enough to say there are rotten apples, you've got to believe it, too. You don't, Inspector, you don't believe it, but I *know*. You've got to accept it from me, or from someone, there's something awful going on. If you don't accept it, if you won't, it means the whole lot's rotten, doesn't it? The whole damn lot's corrupt, it's a corrupt organisation? And that's what people think, they *do*. They think that we're corrupt. You've *got* to see that, you've *got* to!'

Inspector Thompson was still standing. He made an angry gesture with his hand, a gesture telling her to cease. But Sandra had already finished. She gulped. She sat down, heavily. The inspector glared at her.

'Young woman,' he said, clearly. 'I regret to say that I think you are an extremely stupid and arrogant person. Your assessment of this establishment and your colleagues is at once distasteful and absurd. Your assessment of the public attitude is bizarre. I do not think I will pursue this any further.'

'Good,' said Sandra, defiantly. She stood up to go. Her knees were trembling. 'Good. I told you it would be a waste of time.'

As she half turned, Inspector Thompson spoke once more. The note of anger had faded from his voice. He sounded genuinely sorry.

'Yes,' he said. 'Regret. I had already received reports of your behaviour, disturbing reports indeed, that I had hoped would prove inaccurate. Sadly, I can only conclude that they were right. Your sexual misconduct, for example. Whether one puts it down to immorality or immaturity seems hardly to matter any more. Either way, you are clearly unsuited to the job.'

Sandra was rooted to the spot. She turned bright scarlet, her face began to absolutely burn. She opened her mouth to speak, but nothing came. She opened and closed her mouth like a fish.

Inspector Thompson picked her letter from the surface of his desk and held it in his hand. He shook his head.

'Yes,' he said. 'I really am sorry. You must leave this station immediately. Your resignation is accepted.'

NINETEEN

Sandra left headquarters at once, speaking to no one. As she crossed the car yard, Terry moved swiftly through the double doors behind her and caught her up. He was panting slightly, his brow beaded with sweat.

'Where you going, gal?' he said. 'As if I didn't know. You've done it, haven't you?'

Sandra was white-faced still, with shock and fury.

'Yes,' she said, not slowing down at all. 'I'm going to join the human race again. And it's not a minute before time, Terry. It's not a bloody *second*.'

He kept pace with her until they were a couple of hundred yards from HQ. Then he took her arm and stopped her.

'You'll get me shot,' he said. 'Chasing around in my shirtsleeves without me hat on. Talk to me, Sandra. Tell me what happened.'

She tried to pull her arm away, then shrugged. She flashed him an angry little smile.

'Inspector Thompson happened,' she said. 'He gave me some spiel about how good I was, my great future in the force, what a loss I'd be. And when it didn't work he hit me with the Updike line. Not fit to be a copper anyway – because I'm just a tart.'

Terry whistled.

'Wonderful,' he said. 'How did he square up the two halves of your personality, then?'

Sandra gave a short laugh.

'Simple. I didn't agree about the Noor Allahi thing, which proved the stories must be true. I'm immoral. I'm immature, too, of course. Too immature, unfortunately, for the sex thing not to matter. He actually seemed *sorry*, love. It's incredible.'

'Patronising git,' said Terry. 'You should have cracked him one.'

'Yeah,' said Sandra. 'If I hadn't been so surprised I'd have gobbed in his eye. Brian, incidentally, gets no mention. Sex for him is fine, whoever he does it with. And by the way, Noor Allahi probably killed his father after all. And *I'm* immoral! Terry, love, it's a swamp. It's a disaster area.'

'Well, you can't say I didn't tell you the rot came from the top, can you now?' said Terry. 'Not that Thompson's the top yet, thank God, although he's the sort of slimepot to get there in the end. Some minds are closed, gal. You'll find out.' He sighed. 'And another soldier bites the dust.' He sang, almost under his breath: 'And who wants to stay at home? When the freedom fighters are fighting?'

'I'm sorry, Terry,' said Sandra. 'I'm really sorry. You must think I'm an awful coward. But I just couldn't see it in the end. I couldn't see what good I could possibly do. To be quite honest, I can't see that you can help much, either. I think you're on a hiding to nothing in the force.'

A police car drove past, the officers inside it staring at them, puzzled. Terry gave them a wave and Sandra stared them out.

'You might be right, love,' he said. 'But I'm a tenacious sod. While there's life there's hope's my motto. And anyway, I told you. I'm the Lone Ranger. Did you see the paper today? Any of them?'

'No,' said Sandra.

'A 25-year-old African student was dragged off the platform of a bus in London yesterday by a gang of thugs. White, naturally. There were more than ten stab wounds in his body when they left him. Dead. It made one paragraph in the populars and four inches in the *Guardian*. If he'd been white and they'd been black we don't have to guess what would have happened. We know.'

'You sound like my boyfriend talking,' said Sandra. 'My ex. It's horrible, yes, but I still don't see . . .'

'I'm staying in to do the dirty work,' said Terry. 'We need some lunatic to take on the thugs, and pigs, and fascists. We need some lunatic who *wants* to! It's me. Hi Ho Silver.'

'You said last week we were just the infantry,' said Sandra. 'You said it was because of the politicians that these things happen. I believe you, Terry. It terrifies me. So what are you saying now?'

'While there's life there's hope,' said Terry. 'Even politicians are human, a few of them. Even they can learn. It's not too late, even now. I'm not the only good guy, Sandy. There's plenty more Lone Rangers in the force. Remember Tony Gardiner. Think hard about him.'

'Yeah,' said Sandra. 'I'm not so optimistic as you, love. That's all.'

'And you call me a cynic,' he said good-humouredly. 'A bloody teenager talking like the ancient bloody mariner. Listen, love, there's always hope. Even if we go through riots every week and full-scale insurrections. One day they'll be forced to sit up and admit it. Our glorious leaders! And do something positive. It's not too late, I promise you. Even for the fuzz. But I wish, love, how I wish, you hadn't gone.'

'Yeah,' she said. 'I've let you down. I'm just a lousy coward.'

'You're a bloody belter,' said Terry. He laughed. 'You're a bloody marvel, Sandra Patterson, and I love you to your little cotton socks. Bless 'em. I'm going back to work. To fight the good fight. Keep in touch, kid. Don't forget to keep in touch.'

She watched him as he walked back to the station. At the entrance to the yard he turned. He had his handkerchief in his hand, to mop his brow. When he saw that she was still watching, he waved it with a grin. And disappeared. Sandra turned away.

It took a good few days for her family to get used to the idea, but they didn't give her any trouble over it. Her mother was the most upset, naturally, especially as Sandra would not go into details as to why she had left. She assumed that it must be something personal, part of Sandra's tangled love-life – which had been in the forefront of her mind, in any case, for many weeks. She also took to clipping job ideas from newspapers, and presenting them to Sandra in an eager, nervy, way that made her quite impatient for a time. She was worried about her daughter's prospects, and kept dropping heavy hints about nursing. Sandra brushed them off as best she could and told her she was resting. She'd make up her mind soon enough, she said, and she'd get a job all right – her sort always did.

Her father never joined in these sessions, but one afternoon, as they stood in the garden watching one of their good bonfires, just the two of them, he said: 'Have you thought of being a security guard, Sandra? The pay's not all that different, and you'd be doing good, still. I know you want to do that.'

She smiled.

'That would be a cop-out, Dad,' she said. 'No pun intended. I left the police force, if you must know, because I didn't see how I possibly *could* do good, the way they work. It was just wrong for me. But I'm not going to pretend I'm putting the world to rights by protecting some rich swine's property for a nice fat wage. Oh no no!'

He coughed in the smoke.

'Take your point,' he said. 'I take your point. Sorry I spoke.'

For the first time in ages, Sandra read a lot, and following up things that Terry's ideas had suggested, she read a lot of history. Maggie, who spotted the change immediately, was very mocking in a friendly sort of way.

'You're getting to be a real bookworm, my lovely,' she said one night. 'I think it's time you got yourself another feller. Your brain's turning!'

They were sitting outside the Crown and Cushion on the harbourfront, dressed in coats because it was quite chilly.

The sun was low and watery over the port, and Sandra watched the little pale blue ferry as it steamed slowly across the tide.

'Is it hell!' she answered. 'I'm better off without, gal. I've had a bellyful.'

'Impossible,' said Maggie. 'There aren't enough men in the world to ever make me fed up. They're gorgeous. I love the lot of them.'

'Dirty bitch,' said Sandra. 'Now what *would* Roger say!'

'Seriously, though,' said Maggie. 'You haven't half changed a lot, Sandra. Are you unhappy, love?'

Sandra looked into her sister's eyes.

'I'm a bit lost, Mag,' she said. 'I don't know what I'm doing. I don't know what to do.'

'Mm,' said Maggie soberly. 'Well, you're not likely to find out in a book. That I *can* tell you for nothing.'

'I don't know,' said Sandra. 'I'm reading up on Germany at the moment. About the Nazis. I'm fascinated by it. D'you know they murdered six million Jews and the people who lived near the camps said they never heard the screams or smelt the smoke? I'm fascinated by it.'

'You morbid cow,' said Maggie. 'But what's it got to do with you?'

'I'm looking for a way to help, that's all. I'm looking for a way to make somebody listen. To admit it, that's all.'

Maggie drained her gin. She looked puzzled.

'Admit what? What are you talking about, our kid?'

'Oh nothing,' Sandra said. 'I'll go and get another drink. The screams and the smoke, that's all. D'you want some crisps?'

Maggie threw her head back and hooted.

'Smoky bacon, please!' she said.

For two weeks or more, David phoned quite regularly. Sandra spoke to him, she did not try to duck, but she held out no hope for him. He was very insistent, and often got upset. She had been the guilty party, he said, but he was prepared to forgive her utterly, and to forget. He'd never mention Brian Updike again, he promised. Sandra was calm, and patient, and as kind as she could be. She apologised for her behaviour, said she was confused, said her decision to leave the police had upset her badly, and she needed time to think, alone. In the end she said she did not love him any more, she could not help it, that was that. He got desperate, so did she, and finally she hung up. He rang after that, but she would not talk. She was sorry, but it was over. That was that.

One day, to her amazement, Brian phoned. Her stomach turned to water. She feared he was going to abuse her, to utter filth. But he just told her, in a cold, unpleasant way, that he had never loved her. I never even liked you, he went on, and I hope I never see you again. He hung up, and she stood in the hall, white and shaking. It was horrible.

One day Ahmed phoned. He asked her to meet him in the White Swan for a drink.

'Why?' she said, in total surprise. 'No, that sounds rude! But . . . well – why?'

'A cat can look at a queen, can't it?' he laughed. 'Not afraid to be seen out with a jungle-bunny, are you? I'll leave my spear at home, promise!'

'But really,' said Sandra. 'Why, Ahmed? Has David put you up to this? Will he be there?'

'Honest Indian,' said Ahmed. 'Whoops, sorry. I must stop making all these racist jokes! No, David didn't, and he won't. I fancied seeing you, that's all, and buying you a gin.'

'There's another reason, Ahmed. Tell me, for God's sake.'

'You are a hardened cynic, do you know that?' said Ahmed. 'All right. I want to tell you about the new march. For Noor Allahi. I'm going to try to persuade you to come along.'

'To *march*? *Me*? But I. . . . But . . .'

She swallowed. Ahmed chuckled at the other end.

'Ah well, it would have been great publicity,' he said. 'I

expect you'd have needed armour plating and a crash-hat when your ex-buddies recognised you. Never mind. It was just a thought, I'm a fool. See you, love. No hard feelings.'

'Stop!' she said. 'Don't hang up!'

He didn't.

'Yes?' he said. 'I'm still here, Sandra.'

'I . . . Oh, to hell with it. Look, I'm not sure about marching, Ahmed, but I'd like a drink all right. I'd love one. I want to talk. I want to . . . I want to find a . . . Oh, I want to talk, that's all.'

'No problem,' said Ahmed. 'I speak the language like a native! My privilege and pleasure. See you in half an hour, then. I'll wear a big carnation so you recognise me. In case you're colour blind!'

When she had hung up, Sandra shook her head. Ahmed sounded jolly, that was sure. Behaving like a twit. Whatever happened it looked as if she'd have a laugh. She could do with one. Her father came out of the kitchen, on his way upstairs.

'You're looking funny, gal,' he said. 'You look like you've lost your mind.'

'Yeah,' she said. 'Maybe I'm going to find it, though. It wouldn't be before time, I reckon. Listen Dad, I'm going out. I'm going for a drink in town.'

'With a feller? You've got that funny look on. Like you're waking up at last.'

'Yes,' she said. 'With a black man. What d'you make of that?'

He shook his head.

'Bugger all, gal,' he said. 'I've given up trying to make you out, long ago. You're a mystery, Miss. A bloody mystery.'

He set off up the stairs.

'Have a good time,' he said. 'Lock up before you go to bed, gal. See you in the morning.'

'Yeah,' she said. 'Night, love. See you in the morning.'

She went to get her bag and coat.

POSTSCRIPT

Noor Allahi, despite representations to the Home Secretary, marches, and the efforts of the Commission for Racial Equality and two MPs, was deported to Pakistan, after several stays of execution, five months after his rearrest. Blood test evidence that appeared to prove that he was Yusuf Mansoor's son was discounted by the Home Office. The same evidence, that appeared to prove he could not have been the murderer, was apparently accepted by the police. The investigation into Yusuf Mansoor's death continued.

Mrs Mansoor and the two young children continued to live in Tuebrook Road, on social security. The family hoped to be able to save the air fares to Pakistan so that they could rejoin Noor Allahi. A fund was later set up by the REC.

Two formal complaints were investigated by the police. Allegations of brutality and misconduct against the person of Noor Allahi were found to be groundless. Allegations of misconduct at the first protest march were found to be without foundation.

The file on the murder of Yusuf Mansoor remains open, although active investigation has ceased. No one – except Noor Allahi – has ever been arrested.